# Ruby Red and The Wolf

*Robert Wright*

ISBN: 1542441609
ISBN-13: 978-1542441605

Cover design by: Sherrie Wright

# DEDICATION

For all those who fight for the downtrodden.

# CONTENTS

# ACKNOWLEDGMENTS

Thanks to the many people who helped in the creation of this book, your assistance was invaluable. And special thanks to the characters who reside in my mind and let me tell your tales.

## PROLOGUE – THE PROPHECY

Saira could hear the heavy footsteps outside her door and cringed inside while keeping the stony façade of her race plastered on her face. She had, after all these years, been able to distance herself from the touch that her captor forced on her body. Though now she had more than herself to worry about; she had a life growing deep within her that she needed to protect.

The door slammed open, hitting the stone wall then bouncing back toward the opening. Large rough hands grasped the door before it slammed into their owner. She flinched just the slightest at the violence of her captor's entrance. This small reaction brought an evil smile and a chuckle to the rough face that looked at her from the door. "So my lady, am I finally getting through that icy mask of yours?"

She admonished herself for reacting even that little bit, knowing that a creature such as her captor would be able to see even the smallest change in emotions. Saira stepped forward, smelling the liquor fumes that rolled off the being that stood before her. "Though you can take my body without my permission, Marcus, I will never give in to you in spirit. That will always be mine and mine alone. I will never stoop down to being an animal like you, dog."

Marcus looked the slim tall lady up and down and his smile grew. "Yeah, well we have all the time in the world to change your mind, my lady. Sooner or later you will kneel to me as your master."

Saira moved with surprising speed and lashed out with her right hand, connecting with Marcus's face. The strike never even caused Marcus to blink or move and he slowly reached up to rub his hand over the red mark that heated his cheek. "For that, my lady, you will pay dearly. I think maybe I have been too lax in your treatment." The man turned and left the room slamming the door closed behind him.

Saira waited until she could hear the footsteps fade and moved over to her bed and sat down with a small sob. She sat there thinking through all the possibilities for escape not only for her sake but for the new life she carried. She needed to get out soon before her condition became obvious to those around her. If Marcus found out about the baby that she carried within her there was no way that she would ever make it out of this prison alive. The cold stones of her prison with their wards against her magic seemed to mock the tall thin silver-haired women as she looked around the walls and started once more to figure a way out of this hell she was in.

After a few hours of thinking and planning, she lay back on the bed in despair knowing that escape from this place would be hard if not impossible. A large pop sounded in the middle of her room, jerking Saira upright and once more putting that stony look on her face.

As a small cloud of smoke cleared from the center of the room, Saira cracked a minuscule smile at the dragon that stood before her. "Hello Percy, what are you doing here? How did you beat the wards that the mutts placed around my prison?"

The four-foot green dragon wearing a bowler hat and dark black shades bowed before the lady in front of him, the smelly smoke from an old lit cigar curling above his head. "Hello Princess Saira, I have come to take you out of this place. As for the wards that these shifters use, well let's just say that I have had help from a higher power to beat them."

Saira stood looking at the dragon, suspicion clouding her eyes. Dragons, especially this dragon, were not known for meddling in other creature's lives and when they did it usually lead to no good for the unlucky person. "And why, after all this time, would you trouble yourself with my welfare, dragon? And there is no higher power than a fae."

Percy glanced at Saira's middle and then his face softened with a smile. "Why Princess, because you are with child, is there no better reason for me to come get you? As for powers, in this world, there are some powers that even the fae cannot understand, such as the power of the One."

Saira stood there looking down at the dragon as her hands encircled her stomach as though to protect the life within. "I don't know what you are talking about, dragon," she said putting as much scorn as she could into her voice. "As for this One, that is only a stupid myth that humans have made up to feel better about their miserable lives."

The dragon reached up and took the smelly weed that dangled from his jaws, tossed it down to the floor and ground it underfoot. "Sorry, nasty habit and forgot it's bad for the baby." As he looked up at the lady before him the smile vanished. "You are with child, Princess; a child that was conceived between two races. This child will grow up to have all the powers of every race inhabiting Mother Earth and will save the downtrodden from the evil that rules this world. That is why I am here to save you."

Saira felt faint and slowly sank down onto the bed behind her. She glanced at the dragon that now stood there with his arms crossed across his puffed out chest and slowly shook her head from side to side as she whispered, "No, that is not possible, Percy. No race can conceive with another."

The dragon's face once more softened at the young women's fate and walked over to her, laying a hand softly on her arm. "I am sorry, Princess Saira, but it is a dragon prophecy made long ago and cannot be changed. Besides what the One wants, the One gets."

Saira shook the dragon's hand off of her arm and stood, anger flashing in her eyes at the absurdity of the dragon's words. "No, I don't believe you. A fae could never get pregnant from a dog like that. I'm not some bitch that will have his pup. It is my time to bear a child and Mother Earth or the One as you call her has granted me this blessing as she does all the royal fae. That is all there is to it."

Percy hopped up on the bed and took off his hat and laid it next to him. He looked over the top edge of his glasses at the lady before him and shook his head at her denial. "You know deep down within your heart that that is not true, Princess. The great Mother Earth has heard the cries of injustice from her children and has picked you to carry out this task. That child that you carry is a special life that will save countless others when she comes of age. You will need to train her with all the arts that you have at your disposal so that when she is eighteen she will be ready to take her place in this world as its savior."

Saira turned to her would-be rescuer, her anger growing by leaps and bounds at the dragon's words. "I shall not do this, Percy. The first chance I get I will rid myself of this abomination that I carry within me. I will . . ."

Saira's words died in her throat at the wisp of smoke that the dragon held within his hand. As the smoke swirled around his fingers, she could see wispy red hair framing a red-cheeked face within it. "This is the life that you carry, Princess Saira. Though you think it is a burden now you will carry this child to term and love her as best as that icy fae heart of yours can."

Saira gave a small sigh of contentment at the cute, chubby little face that looked up at her from the smoke in the dragon's hand. She whispered, "Such a little thing to carry so heavy a burden on her shoulders."

Percy nodded once and closed his hand and the image of the red-headed child disappeared in a tiny puff of smoke. "Yes, that is why you were given this precious gift. You need to protect her and nurture the child as she grows, but most of all you need to train her for her birthright, and . . ." Percy stopped and frowning and looked down at the floor.

"And what dragon?"

"And," the dragon's voice lowers in volume so that the princess could barely make out what he said. "Your child will have a younger sister. No, not from you though she will be her sister nonetheless. She will also be a gift from the One." Saira looked down at the dragon as he hopped off the bed. His two feet hit the floor forcing a small puff of air from his mouth. She gave a small chuckle as the dragon glanced up at her sideways and peeked out from behind his shades. "Yeah laugh it up, fae, but when you get as old as me it won't be so easy to move either."

The laughter died on Saira's lips as she got a faraway look on her face and she whispered, "I don't think that will be a problem, dragon, for I don't see further into my future than when my child reaches her eighteenth birthday."

Percy looked down at the floor avoiding the fae's look and shook his head. "I'm sorry Princess Saira, I cannot tell you what the One holds for you, but . . ."

Saira gave the dragon a piercing look. "You can't or you won't tell me, dragon?"

"Well, will it help you to know that when I'm needed most I will be at your daughter's side, Princess?"

Saira looked down at the dragon and thought of all the rumors that she had heard about him and his 'help'. "No, not really, dragon."

Percy moved over to the middle of the room, shrugging his shoulders at her answer, as Saira moved next to him. "Damn, forgot my hat," the dragon said as he walked over to the bed once more, popped his hat on his head and returned to Saira's side.

Reaching up, he grabbed the young lady's hand and with the other stuck an unlit cigar in the side of his mouth. With a wide grin, he looked up at Saira and sang out gleefully, "Hang on Princess, it has been a little while since I have used this magic with anyone other than myself." A large pop echoed in the room as the dragon and fae disappeared in a puff of smoke.

OOOOO

Lars and the other two guards with him opened the door of the fae's room and entered. "Alright, Princess you're to come with us and . . ." His voice ground to a halt as he surveyed the empty room.

He glanced back at the other two and saw that their eyes were as large with shock as his probably were. Lars looked around the room at the empty bed and one small dresser that was the only furniture. He sniffed the air, smelling a light odor of smoke that hung in the air. His shoulders slumped as he knew that this was his and his companions last night on this earth, for there was no way that Marcus wouldn't take his anger out on the three of them – whether or not it was their fault the fae had escaped.

"Come on boys, we need to tell Marcus," Lars said with resignation as he closed the door not bothering to lock it behind him.

"But, but shouldn't we search the room? I mean maybe she is hiding in there somewhere, I mean . . ." the youngest of the guards stammered out his protest.

Lars just laughed at the expression the other two guards wore and started to walk down the hall to his fate. "You can search all you want but I'm going tell Marcus that she is gone. The quicker I tell him the quicker I'll get it over with."

The two shifters stared at Lars's back for a second as he walked down the hall, glanced at each other then hung their heads in despair over their luck at having pulled guard duty on the night that their leader's prize passion disappeared. They slowly followed Lars down the hall to face their death.

# THE GREAT ESCAPE

I quietly opened the window of my prison and the smell of freedom floated through on a breeze and ruffled my tangled red hair. Looking out at the late summer night sky I took a deep breath of the air that was just now cooling down from the heat of the day, not that this part of Washington ever got that hot or so I heard. Taking in the clear air, I snapped back to the job at hand while I glanced over the silent backyard and slowly lowered the rope I had hidden in my room to the darkness below me.

Turning, I eased my body out the window trying to make as little noise as I could knowing that my jailer for the last eighteen years could hear a mouse fart fifty feet away. It was only two stories down but, in stealth mode, it seemed to take forever before my feet touched the ground. The rough rope chewed into my hands making me wince as the sweat trickled into the tiny marks made from the bite of its fibers. Damn, why couldn't I have found a better method of escape, I thought, as I gingerly wiped my tender palms against my pants.

"Going somewhere, Ruby dear?" a harsh voice whispered from the shadow of a large pine that grew in the backyard. The rough voice shook me to my core and kicked out all thoughts of the pain from the insignificant marks that decorated my hands from my recent climb.

Damn, why was she out? I thought I had finally beaten the old girl as I turned toward the callous voice that belonged to my jailer. "Why of course not, Mother. What makes you think I was going anywhere?"

As my mother stepped out of the gloom, I looked up at the thin angular face framed by the waist length silver hair dancing in the starlight and reflecting the bright shining light of the moon. Not like the mass of red curls that I fought each morning to tame into some semblance that would please my mother. She looked up at my bedroom window, disappointment lighting her eyes. "So then tell me, Ruby, is this some new exercise routine that we are working on? Oh and in your best outfit too? Interesting. Well, young lady, I'm waiting?"

The sarcasm in my mother's voice and the light tapping of one foot cut deep, leaving me feeling like a little girl again standing beside a broken vase. I looked up into the deepest blue eyes that I had ever seen reflecting their exasperation in my actions once more. "Listen, Mother, I'm eighteen today. I don't think that I should have to stay inside after dark. Besides a boy . . ." I whined as I dropped my eyes to the ground.

"A boy?" the whisper of annoyance I had heard so many times in my life when I hadn't quite measured up to the old gal's standards sounded again.

I looked up from the ground, a little flicker of defiance flaring within my being, my core, looking to rebel against those cold blue eyes of my mother's. "Fine, call him a man, and I'm eighteen and I'm an adult so I can . . ." My voice sputtered to a stop as those eyes just bore deep within me and seemed to freeze that small flare of insolence without a word needed. I dropped my eyes to the ground again as the silence of the night wrapped the two of us in its embrace.

My mother and I lived up in the hills. So very little sound from the town below us crept into our backyard, especially after dark. The night's quietness was broken by the wings of a large owl that glided above our heads looking for its nightly meal. I glanced up at my mother through the unruly tangled mess of my hair and saw that same look on her face as she had before. I swear the old gal could stand as still as a statue forever that look of disappointment written all over her face for anyone to see. Not that we ever had anyone over to our house, mind you.

As the owl flapped away into the night, I heard a quiet sigh of resignation and then felt the light touch of my mother's hand under my chin as she lifted my face up to look at hers. "Ruby, I have not kept you safe for all these years to see you hurt on your coming of age day."

I took a step back from her and her hand released my chin and fell to her side as anger flared within me pushing aside the defiance. "I don't understand what the big deal is. I'm eighteen and I know how to take care of myself. I mean come on Mother; you've had me in private martial arts lessons in every town we lived in since I could stand. And then there is learning how to shoot with any and all weapons made, both legal and illegal, which, by the way, you know I hate with a passion. Then there is the swords, Mother. Swords! I mean who the hell uses a sword nowadays to fight?"

My mother stood there, her arms crossed over her chest as though shielding herself from my anger. I stood there breathing hard from my tirade, waiting for her to strike out with her words or her hands. Again, she stood still as a statue not saying a word, still wearing that hated look on her face. All my life I've strived to once, just once, remove that look to see even a glimmer of approval, but no matter what I never seemed to be able to please my greatest critic, my mother.

It's kind of hard to fight someone that acts like they are right all the time, and just stands there and lets you rant and then points you in the direction they want you to go when they are done with you. As usual, I ran out of steam and my anger died a fast death and was buried right next to the defiance I had shown earlier. I waited in anticipation of the lecture to come. One where she would point out my faults and explain to me why the path I was choosing was wrong.

She just didn't understand that our roads were diverging and that I needed to be set free.

My mother unfolded her arms from across her chest and glided up to me as I once more dropped my head in defeat. We had had this conversation in numerous forms before regarding my freedom, moving, and in the now hated training that my mother insisted on throughout my growing years and always, in one form or another, my mother prevailed in the end. Why had I thought my turning eighteen would change anything, I have no idea.

She glanced at me then back up at the rope hanging out from my bedroom window. "I would suggest that you climb back up that, uhm, exit since you seem so eager for some exercise this evening. Meet me down in the living room where we can figure out a punishment for this indiscretion, Ruby." With that announcement I looked at the rope then back down at my hands and with a resigned sigh I started back up the rope toward my room. Of course, since I wasn't trying to be quiet, the climb up was quicker than the climb down. Or maybe the noise of my feet knocking on the side of the house was my little way of annoying my mother. Once I reached the window, I looked down as my mother looked up at me and she impatiently snapped her fingers at me.

I walked over to the bed, untied the rope, and with a quick fling, I chucked it out the window. I listened to it hit the ground and with a small feeling of satisfaction I heard a small growl of frustration from outside. I knew that I would pay for that little bit of disrespect, but what the hell I was already in trouble. I mean what more could the old gal do to me, right? Walking over I slammed the window closed and then walked down the steps to meet my fate with a light heart.

OOOOO

"One hundred and ninety-eight . . ." Man, I can't believe what an idiot I can be sometimes. "One hundred and ninety-nine . . ." I could barely feel my arms anymore as I counted off the last of the pushups, and I won't even tell you how much my legs were crying out in pain after three hours of my mother's punishments. "Two hundred. . ." Why is it that I keep forgetting that every time I think that I am getting back at the old gal she makes me pay tenfold, I thought, standing up to see her smug smile.

She stood and looked me up and down with some satisfaction. "There Ruby dear, I think that little exercise time will cure any restlessness you have, don't you?"

I glared up into those eyes for a second then back down to the ground and muttered, "Yes, Mother." Every fiber of my being aching and screaming in anguish from her 'little' punishment.

I could feel the presence of my mother as she closed within inches of me and she laid a long thin hand lightly on my shoulder. "You know Ruby I only do this for your own good, to protect you from the bad things that roam the night in this world. My daughter, you are destined for great things one day, but you must learn that you need to think of others and not of yourself, dear." Yeah, like I haven't heard that every night since I was a little girl. Always the same thing, I'm here on this earth for a purpose but never do I hear what that purpose is. A girl can only listen to so much of that drivel before it starts to wear thin. "And besides now that your coming of age day is here, I will explain to you why I have been so careful and protective of you and, yes, I know very hard on you all these years."

I looked up hopefully figuring that, at last, I would get some answers to why my mother had picked us up in the middle of the night and moved us from town to town every couple of years, sometimes every couple of months. All the while having me training in various martial arts, and weapons, but then she gave a little sniff of the air around us. Her nose crinkling at the smell that emitted off my body from a couple of hours of hardcore exercise. "But I think that can wait until tomorrow, Ruby. For now, how about you go and shower and then hop off to bed. We will talk tomorrow about those things I have mentioned."

I dropped my head once more to stare at the floor in frustration, but my mother was right. I needed a shower to wash away the stink from the punishment that she had run me through since I still had plans for this night, plans that my mother knew nothing about or at least so I hoped.

I slowly walked up the steps following my mother down the hallway until she reached her room and turned toward me. I kept my eyes focused on the floor in defeat and mumbled a quick goodnight in response to her own and the quick peck on the cheek. As I headed down to my room, I caught the snick of the lock on my mother's bedroom door and my pace quickened toward my own.

I stripped out of the sweaty clothes, hopped in the shower attached to my room, and gave myself a fast scrub while going over all that had happened tonight in my first escape attempt. Yes, I know that, to some, my mother may be harsh and cold-hearted, but I know that deep down she really does worry and love me and has my best interests at heart. It's just that after growing up as I have with all the late night moves, leaving friends and having no one but my mother around to talk to I just thought that once I turned eighteen it would be different. But this first attempt at escape showed me that nothing had changed and that I needed to take charge of my own life and live it how I wanted. Granted as I had seen earlier this was not going to be easy. But hell if the old gal had taught me anything it was that you had to fight for what you wanted in life because nobody was going to hand it to you on a silver platter.

Hopping out of the shower and throwing on some sweats, I heard a creak from the old wood floors outside my bedroom door as though a weight had shifted. Looking down at the bottom of the door, I could see a slight shift in the light as a shadow moved away. Man, the old girl really doesn't trust me I thought as I closed my eyes with a smile. I let sleep enfold me into its sweet dreams.

OOOOO

My eyes popped open as the chirping of my alarm sounded in the dark night. I pushed the button quickly cutting the sound off in mid chirp. Lying there I listened to the sounds of the house to see if that insignificant noise had awakened my mother. Though all I could hear was the creaking of the house like an old man settling in for the night.

Now let's see if my plan works as I ease myself out of bed and reach over to a basket that held the clean clothes that I had 'forgotten' to put away that day. I dressed as fast as I could, all the while thinking that, hopefully, this was the one time that I got something over on the old girl. If not then I was probably in for a long night of more punishment. Well no, as I looked at my watch, I saw that it was now one o'clock in the morning so I guess it wouldn't really be a long night as much as a long morning if I got caught this time. I stretched, driving the kinks and aches from my earlier punishment out of my body going over all I needed to do to affect my real escape.

Sneaking over to the window once I was dressed, I peeked out at the backyard but saw only the early morning moonlight that danced around the flowers and trees of the fenced yard. Well, so far so good as I moved toward the bedroom door and held my breath as I eased it open on well-oiled hinges. My shoes tied around my neck while my stocking feet made quiet whispers on the wood floor beneath me.

And how do I know that they are well-oiled hinges you may ask? Well, probably because I had laid some oil on them just this morning as my mother worked out in the front garden. Yeah, I figured I would probably get caught the first time, but, hopefully, I would dodge my mother's wrath and skip out tonight to do something I had never done before: meet with a boy. I felt a small shiver of anticipation then paused to collect my thoughts for the upcoming escapade. Like I said before, when you are constantly on the move you leave any friends behind. Then after awhile you just don't bother making friends anymore because you know that sooner or later they'll be left behind again. But tonight was going to be different if I had any say in the matter.

I slid along the upstairs wall where I knew the floor was more solid. Pausing outside of my mother's bedroom with bated breath, standing there listening to the night clamor of our old house. I slowly focused on the noises and tuned out each sound until I was locked on the steady breathing of the person on the other side of the door; a nifty little trick that the old gal taught me. I smiled to myself as I thought how pissed she would be at my using her stealth training to escape her dominance over me.

I could tell by the rhythm of her breathing and the quiet murmurs she sometimes makes in her sleep that the old gal was truly out like a light and it was time to put my plan into action. Yes, I had practiced this little technique before, late at night just to make sure that I would be able to use it for just such of an occasion.  I shuffled my feet along the wall after a minute more of listening until I came to the banister that framed our steps from the second floor to the first.

Now came the tricky part of this whole operation I thought as I eased my leg over the banister and slowly slid down the slick wood to the floor below me. I had practiced this move too, numerous times before because I knew no matter how careful I was the steps would give me away. It seemed that no matter where I stepped on them there was the tiniest of creaks. My butt hit the large round ball at the bottom of the banister and I slowly slid off, my stocking feet kissing the ground floor of our house. Once again, careful preparation like all that extra polishing of the banister made the difference.

Moving like a ghost toward the front door, grateful that this house had yet to have an alarm system installed on all the entrances as had the other houses we had lived in. We had just moved into this place over the weekend and my mother was a little vexed that she hadn't been able to get someone out here right away to do her bidding. As you can see, I wasn't the only one is this world that disappointed my mother, but I was the one that seemed to excel at it the most. Besides she tended to look down at all people and see their failures rather than their possibilities, guess that was just her nature.

As I thought about it, I figured what did she expect since this hick town wasn't like Seattle where we had been living? In fact, I had been a little surprised that we had moved only about two hours north of Seattle, not that we had lived there long mind you. Usually, when we move from one place to another it's across the country and not just up the road from where we were, and not in small towns like this one. But with my mother you never knew where you would end up at from one day to the next.

The front door opened on another set of well-oiled hinges, I know I'm such a little sneak, just enough for me to slip through into the now cool night air. I heard the quiet click of the door lock and I paused before I slipped the key out of the door and into my pocket. Turning I scanned the road outside our house for any movement before I silently moved down the porch steps. Sitting on the bottom steps figuring that it was safe, I put my shoes on before heading off to my early morning rendezvous.

Maybe it was because I was so keyed up or that I still expected my mother to jump out from the bushes that grew along the front porch, but some noise or maybe a movement caught my attention as I tied my shoes. I stopped and looked up into the early morning darkness and waited for whatever attracted my attention, but the only noise in the night was the swish of the owl that flew overhead. Waiting a few more seconds, I shrugged my shoulders and figured that my imagination was just running overtime. With a little chuckle and smile at my nerves, I hopped up from the porch steps and with the thought that I had finally outsmarted the old girl at her own game I hurried down the road to my first date. This was definitely going to be a night that I remembered.

OOOOO

As the girl moves down the road into the moonlit morning, a lone figure steps out from the trees in front of the old gray house. Reaching up toward his ear, the large dark shadow presses a small switch and whispers, "She is leaving now. Are you sure that you don't want us to take her too, Red One?" Listening to a quiet voice, he then nods to himself at the answer received. "Roger, understood. Will follow the plan, out." The shadow reaches down to a radio on his hip and flips a switch to move to another channel and once more reaches up and pushes the small switch and whispers, "All Red units, Subject One has left the house. We go in one half hour."

There are several clicks at his command then silence in the dark as the shadow starts to move back under the cover of the trees, but stops at the whisper of sound that carries on the night breeze. He sniffs the air while searching the night around him for any danger. Then, after a few seconds, quietly moves back under cover. He thinks back to his orders and wonders why they just didn't take the two of these creatures while they had them both in one place, but in his organization you didn't argue or question orders, if you wanted to live that is.

He looks down at his watch to check the time once more and smiles, at least this operation would finally be over. It had taken eighteen plus years, but now it would be done and hopefully the organization could move on.

OOOOO

The two pair of eyes looking through night glasses divides their attention between the young girl and the barely hidden shadow under the trees. Michael takes a shallow breath at the discovery of one of his enemies and starts to scan the night for the others that had to be there in hiding, for these creatures, he knew, always traveled as a pack.

The younger man beside him shifts and sighs from the long night of staying in one place on the hunt. Michael, the older and more experienced of the two, quickly shifts back to the shadow of the creature he had spotted and watches as the shifter pauses for a few seconds then melts into the darkness under the trees. Michael gives the one beside him a glare then resumes looking around for the others he was told would be here.

The younger man doesn't say a word at the quiet rebuke for he knows that one small screw up on a night like tonight and he would never live to see the sunrise. After a couple of minutes, the older man taps him on the shoulder and the two move down the hill that they had been on most of the night as quietly as possible.

They trek down an old deer path and around another hill that takes them into the housing complex where they had parked their truck earlier. Without a word, the two pack their equipment into protective bags and climb into their vehicle and head down the road toward the main part of town.

"Sorry about that back there, Michael, I just . . ." the younger man whispers even now in the moving truck as they drive away from danger

Michael just waves his hand cutting off his apology as he glances over at the youngster driving. "You only get one chance with those creatures, boy. You got me?"

The younger man glances at Michael and nods his head at the lesson learned. "Yeah I understand, but what was the point of us being there if we weren't going to take them out and save that lady and her daughter?"

Michael sits back in his seat, a small smile slipping onto his face as he gives a little chuckle. "I just wanted to see if it was true that new Supers had moved into Bellingham. We don't get in the way of Supers killing other Supers, boy.

"You mean that lady and the girl were . . ."

Michael nods at the younger man's question and smiles some more. "Yeah let them kill each other off; just means less for us when the time comes to rid this world of their kind."

The younger man sits up straighter and nods at the older man's words even though it went against everything he believed in as a police officer. But Michael was right; a couple less Supers in the world wouldn't hurt humans, that was for sure.

# COLD IRON KILL

I moved down the road, stopping every once in awhile to get my bearings. It really sucked being in a new town and not being sure of your way around, even with a place this small. Stopping at the bottom of the hill, I looked around at the quiet streets of Bellingham and thought that this definitely wasn't Seattle or Chicago. Seems like the streets rolled up and everything closed down by midnight, yeah the small town life, I sighed, just got to love it.

After another hour of walking, I was finally moving down the street that led to a small park that hung between the edge of the ocean and the city itself. I couldn't wait to meet my new friend, well actually I don't know if we were friends or what since I had only met him yesterday while I was out picking up cleaning supplies for the old house, but you know a girl can wish, can't she? A quick glance at my watch and I saw that I had made pretty good time for it had only taken me an hour and a half of walking to make it this far; guess all that working out my mother had me do since I could stand on my own two feet was worth something after all.

I know, meeting someone you just met at two-thirty in the morning in an isolated area isn't the brightest idea, but when you feel a connection with someone you just have to go with what feels right. And right now meeting with this boy feels right, no matter what my mother would think about the whole situation. It was just time for me to be free, to be on my own and to follow my whims and my heart.

Of course, the trouble I'll be in if my mother wakes up and tracks me down will make that little punishment earlier tonight pale in comparison, but you know what I'm tired of having the old girl run my life. Just because she has no man of her own doesn't mean I can't go out there and meet someone new.

Walking down the curving road past the condominiums above and crossing the railroad tracks, I ducked under the gate entering Boulevard Park where my new life would start. I can see the building where I was to meet my new 'friend' as I took in the sweet smell of the ocean with deep breaths of pleasure. I hurried over to the structure in anticipation, hoping that he hadn't left yet for I saw I was a couple minutes late. "Jason," I whispered into the silent night.

It's so quiet right now in the park, all I can hear are the waves as they lap at the rocks that line the shore and some soft music winding its way down to the park from some open window nearby. Then another noise in the night coming from the side of the building makes me peer into the darkness. "Jason?" I whisper once more, a trace of fright sounding in my voice as I hope with all my heart that it isn't my mother out there in the night.

A low, rough voice whispers my name from the dark making my heart skip a beat at the sound. "Ruby?" Moving toward the shadow that detaches from the side of the building, I'm suddenly standing in front of the one that I came to see this night. I look Jason over. Like I said, a boy I had just met yesterday. Well no, not a boy at all, I mean his six feet towers over my little five-seven frame. Of course in the moonlight, I could just see the shorts and tight shirt he wore and I knew that he definitely did not have the body of a boy. Steady girl, I thought, as I eyed my new friend once more. I mean you just met this guy yesterday. But my heart gives a little patter in anticipation for this night. Damn with all my mother's training why is it she never told me what to do in this kind of situation.

I stood there looking over at him, the one who had invited me out to this secret late night date until he gave me a confident smile and took my hand in his. "I'm so glad that you could get out, Ruby. Come on, I brought us a little morning snack. We can eat, maybe talk a little and get to know each other," he whispered as he pulled me down a short path and around the building to hide us from any prying eyes. Once more my body gave a little shudder and it wasn't from the cool breeze that flowed from the ocean waves.

Yeah, I thought, eat just what I wanted to do with this guy in front of me. Then a nervous little giggle slipped out as we moved over to some tables that were set out in front of the building. The ocean lapping at the rocks covered the sound thankfully or Jason seemed not to notice as he led me to a table that had a small candle lit on it and a basket lying alongside it. Damn not only was this guy drop dead gorgeous, but he was romantic as well. I gave a small sigh of contentment as he held my chair out for me and I slid into the seat. Oh yeah, this was going to be the best night of my life and I didn't care one bit what happened to me when I got home in the morning.

OOOOO

The shadow man moved out from the trees and looked down as another moved up to his side. This shadow though moved silently on four legs instead of two. It sniffed the air and then nudged the arm of the man. "I know, it's almost time to attack but we follow orders and he said no one goes in alone." The wolf whined and then gave a low growl. "Well if you want to disobey Marcus you go ahead. The rest of us wait five minutes more."

The wolf glances up, baring his teeth at the man and then whines again, but stays right by the side of the leader of this operation to wait the next five minutes knowing that any disobedience in the organization means instant death.

OOOOO

Saira slowly opened her eyes and listened to the darkness of the late summer night. The old house creaked and settled as the early morning cold seeped into its old bones. She lay there filtering out all the little noises of the night now seeking out the gentle breathing of her daughter, Ruby.

The absence of that breath, that she had listened to for eighteen years, told her that the most precious gift she had been given in her long life was no longer in the house. Saira leaped from the bed in a long developed fear. A fear that Marcus had finally come and taken the one good thing that he had ever given her. As Saira moved down the hallway, she paused outside Ruby's bedroom door. Her thoughts racing, no it wouldn't be him, for if it had been he would have never left her alive. She had defied him all these years by hiding the one thing that the shifter wanted most in this world and he would have avenged himself on her.

She quietly opened the door and peeked inside; she saw that her daughter was really gone. As her heart sinks, she steps into the room and looks, really looks around, and knows that she was right – the girl had left on her own. A small sigh of relief catches in her throat as she spots a minute movement outside the bedroom window. In an instant, she knows that he has found her at last and is happy in a small way that Ruby is not here to face this danger. But damn, if I get out of this, she thinks, I will skin that girl alive. With that decided, she moves to prepare for her enemies.

OOOOO

A soft alarm chimes and the man once more reaches up and pushes the small button. "All teams move in, and remember she doesn't leave the house alive." Three teams of men and wolves move toward the back door while another two meet the leader at the front of the house. The leader stands back as the first two teams break through the front door and move inside for the kill, the crew leader knows that the same procedure was being duplicated in the back of the old house.

OOOOO

Saira moves out of her daughter's bedroom and toward her own. Reaching under the bed, she pulls out an old companion, a short sword of pure silver, and smiles at the thought of what this weapon will do to those that invade her home. The smile then turns to sadness as she wishes that she had shown more love to the one that has kept her going all these years as it looks like she was going to be leaving this iron-kissed world tonight. But deep down she knows that for all her harshness this was what she was preparing her Ruby for – to live without her. And for one of her race, that is sometimes the only love that can be given.

She stands quietly and hears the padded feet of two wolves silently move up the stairs, but knows that there are more waiting for her if she gets by these two. Her trim body crouches down in anticipation of the first attack from her foes. With a small evil grin, she thinks that she will show these mongrels just what one of her royal lineage can do to ones such as these.

Two pairs of eyes glow in the moonlight thrown from the window, and snarls issue from throats that hunger for her blood from the shadowed bedroom doorway. "Well don't just stand there, come and die, boys," she whispers then the first wolf leaps.

She ducks under the leaping form and the sword slices along the underside of the wolf, opening him from throat to tail. The already dying wolf lands on the bed, gasping out its last breaths as his insides spill out on the still-warm blankets.

She doesn't hesitate and over the dying whimpers of the first wolf, she steps forward and with a quick slash, there is the sound of the second wolf's head hitting the floor. Those still down below hear mad laughter and then a yell from above, "IS THAT ALL YOU HAVE TO TRY AND KILL ME WITH, PUPS? YOU'LL NEED SOMETHING BETTER THAN THIS TRASH TO KILL THE LIKES OF ME."

The leader snaps his fingers and points at the two men whose companions are now lying dead upstairs. Both men quickly pull out weapons of their own and charge up the stairs. There is silence as they reach the upper floors then the sound of thumping as their two heads bounce down the stairs to lie at their leader's feet.

"TWO MORE, HOW MANY MORE OF YOU FLEA BITTEN DOGS ARE DOWN THERE?" the crazed voice sounds once again in the silence that follows.

The leader looks down at the two heads and then decides that Plan A wasn't working as his boss said it wouldn't. Well, he knew that he would pay for that mistake when they got back to the organization, but right now the important thing was to finish the mission so onto Plan B.

The leader glances around at the assets that are left, snaps his fingers and everyone in the group moves out of the house. Well, the leader thinks, there was one than one way to take care of an old woman of her kind.

She stood in the bedroom door after beheading the two that had come up the stairs with their man-made weapons. She thinks back to when her daughter had asked what good the swords were in a fight. Was that only a little while ago? Well, I guess I taught at least four of my enemies what good that kind of training was for she thought with a small chuckle. Then with a small sigh and smile, she thinks back to when her daughter was younger and the times that the two of them had sparred together. She had felt great pride in watching her daughter become a warrior in her own right. Saira shakes her head and the image disappears as she focuses on the job at hand.

She stands there listening for what her enemies will do next, for she knows deep down in her heart that he would not let her live for what she has done to him. Slowly moving toward the stairs, listening for the slightest sound from the next attack, a movement from the bed draws her attention and she can see the struggling wolf that she had disemboweled earlier trying to fight death from the silver-induced wounds.

Walking over with a mad grin on her face, she looks down on the wounded creature. There is no pity within her as she knows she would receive none if the situation was reversed. With a swift downward sweep, the creature's head lands on the floor next to its companion's and without a backward glance, she moves back to her bedroom door to once more listen for the enemies' next move.

Standing there, she wonders just what these pups are up to now. Then her mind wanders back to the first time she had come to this new world. She remembers how her own mother had warned her about the dangers of this world of iron, but she had a job to do and came anyways filled with a strange curiosity.

After she had caught Marcus's eye, no matter how hard she tried she couldn't escape his unwanted attention. Then she thought of the horrors of her capture and the way that he used her for his own wicked pleasures. After awhile she withdrew into herself, not fighting his demands and he lost interest.

She had all but given up trying to escape and, if not for the child growing inside of her, she might have given up on life itself. Even now she wasn't sure how two different species like Marcus and her could have reproduced. She still didn't totally believe in the prophecy, no matter what that damn dragon told her. And the whole bull that he tried to lay on her about her child being a gift from the One or Mother Earth as her race called her was still hard to swallow. After helping her escape to freedom, that dragon had just dumped her into this new world with little regard for either her or her unborn child. She had to wonder, if her child had been so damn important to this world why hadn't she seen or heard from Percy in eighteen years.

At the beginning of her new life, her thoughts grew dark and the temptation to go home became almost overwhelming. With the child growing inside of her, she knew that going home would only bring shame. Among her kind, justice would be swift – being used by one such as Marcus, even if that attention had been forced on her would bring death for her and her unborn. So she moved from one spot to another, soon forgetting the image that the dragon had shown her of the unborn child she carried. Her dark thoughts turned to ending the monster's life that would rise from her womb. But the first sight of the full head of red hair and the light brown eyes that, in a certain light, shone with a golden brilliance washed those dark thoughts away. Instantly all thoughts of going home were overridden by the all-consuming desire to protect her child from all the evil that this world could throw at them.

Ever since that day she had been on the run, especially when Marcus found out that they had created a life together. Then he pulled out all the stops to find her and his daughter, having his organization follow and track them down. Hounding them across the country from one end to the other, for somehow Marcus had found out that their child would be special, with powers all her own, and he wanted total control of her.

A cold feeling snapped her back to the present and made her move toward the steps that lead down to the front door. That feeling of iron, the one thing that could kill her kind, but already she was too late as she started down to meet her enemies.

OOOOO

The three men stood there, their special weapons raised to their shoulders aimed at the front door of the house. As the leader saw a slight movement at the bottom of the stairs, he yelled and three flashing streaks reached out toward the old building.

The three special government-made warheads were made of a mix of cold iron and explosives. These were specially made to kill her kind. The warheads streaked through the door and all landed within inches of where Saira stood. The fire washed over her, but it was the iron shrapnel that sent her over to the other side.

The shifters watched as the old house quickly caught fire, knowing that this part of their job was now finished after all this time. The group dispersed to their vehicles to complete one more simple task tonight. Behind them, the old wood of the house was consumed by the flames eating through the walls and they soon collapsed burying Saira's body as the roof came down. A thin shadow detached itself from the dark and looked at the vehicles leaving the area. She had been too late to save the mother, but hopefully not too late for the daughter.

OOOOO

Jason and I talked and ate the simple meal that he had packed for our first date. Even the cool morning air wafting off the ocean couldn't ruin this first of our many nights together. Sitting here at the table of the closed coffee shop in the dark looking up at the stars, I thought that this night couldn't get any better than it was now. Here I sat with someone that really listened to me, not like my mother who dismissed everything I said as silly. God, could I be falling in love after a couple hours?

Of course, that's when Jason's phone rang. He slipped the phone out of his pocket and looked down at the screen that was turned away from me and whispered, "Sorry Ruby I really need to take this. I'll just be a sec."

Moving over to the railing and two tables down, I watched as Jason's shoulders sagged as though a great weight had pushed them down. It only lasted a second then he straightened up and quickly glanced in my direction. As he walked back toward me, I noticed that his face seemed to change as he got closer. Almost as though I was looking at someone other than the person that I had been talking to and falling in love with. He stopped in front of me and a strange smile crossed his face as he said, "Well seems that there has been a change of plans, Ruby."

I looked around the area then back at Jason with some confusion. "What's wrong? What change of plans?"

Jason glanced around and then back at me. "Well it seems like I won't have as much time with you as I wanted, so we will just have to do this quick."

"What. . ." was all I got out before I was flying over the table behind me. I felt myself hit the short metal fence and for a second the night went darker as I started to pass out.

It was the growl from Jason that brought me back. As my vision cleared, I could see him walk toward me, tossing the tables and chairs sitting in his way to the sides. Some went flying over the metal railing while the others flew through the glass windows of the closed coffee shop.

Before I could gather my wits about me and get up and run, Jason pounced on me like a cat on a mouse and had me pinned down on the hard concrete. The wind was knocked out of me and all I could do was stare up at the strange glowing eyes of the boy that minutes ago I had thought of as my soul mate. The hard ground was grinding into my skin where my shirt had ridden up on my back. "You're lucky little girl, for if Marcus didn't want you in one piece I would eat you up," Jason whispered as drool dripped from distended teeth I hadn't noticed before. And when did he get so hairy, I wondered as I glanced at the arms that held me pinned down to the ground?

As all this flashed through my mind, Jason just smiled and lowered his mouth toward my lips all the while grinding his lower body into me while growling once more, "Oh yes, we are going to have a little fun before the others get here, little girl."

Oh, gross was all that crossed my mind as I struggled. More drool slipped out of his mouth and covered my face. My movements seemed to excite him even more than before and Jason suddenly threw his head toward the heavens and howled like a damn wolf. That stopped my struggles for just a second and my blood froze at the sound.

My training kicked in and I did the one thing that all my instructors had taught me to do in this kind of situation. I shifted to the right slightly and then brought my knee up straight into Jason's crotch cutting off his howl mid-sound. The howl became a gurgle and then a whimper and I would have laughed out loud if not for the seriousness of the circumstances.

Pushing Jason off of me and jumping up, I was mad as hell and as he curled up in the fetal position with his hands reaching for his balls. My boots connected with his chin, sending the back of his head into the hard stone at the base of the fence surrounding the seating area with a very satisfying crack.

I didn't wait around to see what damage I had done to him,

but turned and headed out to the park's path. I just knew that something was very wrong and I needed to get home. I had gotten about ten steps away from Jason when I heard that strange growl once more and slowly turned back to look where I had left him. The way his head had hit there was no way that he should be awake, but I got an even bigger surprise as I turned.

Looking back at me was the biggest dog that I had ever seen in Bellingham. Oh, who was I kidding, that was no dog it was a wolf where only seconds ago my old boyfriend had lay my mind clicked and jabbered in panic. I wasn't sure what was going on tonight, but whatever it was the thought flashed through my mind that this is where the heroine comes up with some magical way to kill the scary monster in front of her, but for the life of me my mind just went numb with fright and said bye-bye.

The wolf stood there, his eyes gleaming with hatred as I slowly bent down and reached for a chair that set on its side next to me. "Jason? Is that you? You're not mad because of that little tap I gave you between the legs, are you? Or that little love tap in the head?" The wolf let out another low growl; yeah I think he was pissed.

It took another step closer to me, as I wrapped my hand around the metal back of the chair, growling and showing fangs that I knew would rip my tender skin to little pieces in seconds if given a chance. So yeah, definitely pissed. I guess kicking a boy there really hurts more than his pride so you shouldn't expect him to thank you for it. However, turning into a wolf was taking it to the extreme a little my mind jabbered at me.

Well, tough I thought as I stood up, the chair beside me my only weapon against an angry wolf. Then that anger and defiance that I had felt earlier with my mother came boiling to the surface in a rush. Yeah, I had gotten in a few good shots on Jason, but he deserved each one for the way he had tricked me and then treated me afterward.

Then all of sudden the one thing that had been blocked out of my mind came screaming back to the forefront. If this wolf was Jason then that meant he was a werewolf. I gave a small chuckle then a squeak as my mind tried to wrap itself around that thought on this dark summer night. I looked at the creature before me inching closer as I slowly backed up and coming up against the wall behind me. "Jason, is that really you?" I whispered. The wolf bared its fangs once more and I saw as it stepped forward that it did so a little gingerly as though it hurt a bit in the nether regions. Yep, this monster was Jason alright and he wanted more than he had been after before if that evil look in his eyes meant anything.

Then my mind protested once more – no way, there was no way that this was happening in some small college town like Bellingham. I mean come on, the whole idea of someone turning into a monster, a werewolf, was the silliest thing that could ever happen to anyone. Then the wolf growled once more with slobber dripping from its fangs. Yeah, that was Jason alright as I watched a small of drool form on the ground. God, boys could be so disgusting, especially when they turn into wolves.

Of course, the way my luck had been running tonight, I didn't get long to think about the situation for it was right then that the wolf or Jason or whatever that thing was standing in front of me launched itself at my tender throat. I raised the chair in front of me for protection, but the weight of the massive wolf took me down to the ground. I felt the claws of the creature trying to dig into the concrete so that it could get those sharp fangs ripping into my neck, but the ornamental design of the chair kept him at bay for a few seconds.

I'm not sure how I did it, but with a piercing scream I pushed with all the power I could muster and flipped the chair and wolf off to the side where they crashed into a table and then into the fence surrounding the coffee shop. As I gathered myself and got my feet under me, I was pretty impressed with the strength of the throw especially when I saw the bent bars of the fence that the wolf had hit. I don't think the wolf was as impressed though as it was impaled on one of the bottom bars and was struggling to get itself loose. Well, that looked like it hurt, but I didn't give a damn right that second as I tried to catch my breath.

I leaned back against the wall behind me and stared at the ground taking in a few deep gulps of air and figured that I had dodged having my tender body used as puppy chow and really needed to get out of the park and back home. I looked up as I heard a gross sucking sound in front of me.

My eyes nearly popped out of my head as I watched the wolf pull himself off the fence that had impaled him, stand and shake the blood out of his fur. What the hell these damn things don't die easily.

In fascination, I saw the hole in its side start to close up and as those eerie weird eyes once more turned my way, I could swear I saw the thing smile. The coolness factor was outweighed by the realization that I was in real trouble now as there didn't seem to be a way to kill this nightmare creature. Thinking back to all the horror movies that I had seen growing up what I really, really wished for, was that silver bullet that the hero of the film always seemed to have about now, actually any weapon right now would do I thought glancing around the area.

# SHANE

The dark shadow moved through the street ahead of the three vehicles, knowing that it would be easier to take care of the attackers before they got to the daughter. She stood in the middle of the intersection watching the vehicles approach at full speed.

Hopping up in the air before the first vehicle reached her, she flung a pair of small round objects at the front window shattering the glass and engulfing the passenger compartment in silver flames. The SUV jumped the curve and ran into the large window of a nearby bank, shattering and throwing deadly shards of glass all over the sidewalk and the interior of the building. The screams and howls of the vehicle's occupants mercifully ended when the black truck exploded bringing the front of the bank down on it and crushing all within.

The destruction of the first vehicle and the bank's jarring alarm cover the screeching of tires as the organization's other two vehicles scream to a stop. The shadow turns her back to the flames, knowing that no one is walking away from the devastation and readies to face her next foes.

The leader, watching from the last vehicle, knows that they don't have time for this kind of distraction and radios for the two in the leading vehicle to take care of their unexpected foe. They leap out of the SUV, each taking a step toward their ancient nemesis. The darkness covers the quick movement of their foe and they stumble to a halt, with surprised looks on their faces, as two silver disks appear in the center of their foreheads dropping them instantly. They are dead before they even hit the ground. The shadow, with a quick smile, pulls out a small black box and pushes a red button. A little explosion from the disks buried in each head decapitates them. No sense in taking any chances with these creatures she thinks as she tosses the black box to the side, steps back, and focuses on the last black SUV.

The leader sits there for a second, the frustration washing over him at the loss of so many assets. He knows that he will have to account for every missing shifter with his own blood, even if he successfully returns with Marcus's daughter. The wolf next to him whimpers as they both stare out the windshield at the figure standing between them and their prize. "Yeah, I know the fae has no right to interfere here. So we need to send this bitch to the other side."

He opens the vehicle's door and reaches down between the seats, unlocking a special weapon. "Come on, I think we need to teach this abomination a lesson. Their kind needs to learn to stay out of the way of their betters." He slips out of the truck with the wolf right behind him.

Watching the petite figure backlit by the flames now engulfing the bank, the two shifters move toward the front of the vehicle where the leader stops and cocks the weapon. This little trash may have taken the other four by surprise, but now he has the advantage in this fight. "THIS IS YOUR ONLY WARNING, FAE. THIS IS NOT YOUR FIGHT! LEAVE OUR TERRITORY NOW AND NO HARM WILL COME TO YOU!"

The shadow appears to ignore the warning and for a second stands there in silence. Then, softly, a gentle laugh floats through the night air further infuriating the leader. Then she moves toward the two at a run as the leader takes aim and pulls the trigger of the weapon he holds. Tracers from the weapon fly through the air. In stunned disbelief the leader watches the creature dodge the hail of iron death and then she jumps over his head and lands behind him.

Before he can turn, he feels a burning pain in his chest and as he looks down he sees the silver tip of a sword protruding from it. He gasps, "How. . ." But he never gets to finish that statement, as the creature behind him pulls the sword back with a quick rip. As he starts falling to the ground, he feels another cutting pain at his neck and his head rolls into the street. While the light in his eyes dims, he sees that he is looking at the headless body of his companion lying next to his own body, and then it goes dark.

The shadow slowly looks around at the death and destruction she has caused as her ears tune in to the sirens of the humans coming toward the scene around her. A light-hearted smile plays across her lips, it has been a long time since she had been unleashed on this kind. At least some revenge was enacted tonight. Her thoughts turn to the old house and the figure within it as her smile disappears in sorrow. With one more look around, she turns and moves off toward where the daughter is.

OOOOO

That wolf stands there waiting, for what I don't know but it was starting to royally piss me off. I could feel my anger coursing throughout my body once more and took a step toward that mangy creature, baring my own teeth and growling at the overgrown mutt. "Come on, you think you want to eat me you stupid dog? Well, come and get me." I know, it's pretty stupid for an unarmed girl to challenge a creature like the one that stood before me, but for a minute it seemed to confuse the wolf. It sort of slunk down and tucked its tail between its legs as though it was afraid of me, but even in that submissive stance, the creature was huge.

I was so surprised at its reaction that my feet, of their own accord, took a few steps toward the menacing creature when I felt the power seeping off of it. All I can say was that I felt wildness, a longing to run in the woods, to be free of the city that confined me, and it seemed to be coming from the creature. I looked at the wolf and could picture within my head the feeling of the hunt, the wild chase after prey that had no chance to escape its mighty power.

Slowly I raised my arms toward that power, that feeling I wanted so bad. A wild magic, for want of a better word, that I could almost taste, I wanted to have that feeling deep within my own body flowing through me all for my own. Then I could feel it. I could feel that power, leaking from the creature before me and into my body, flowing into my blood. That's when the wolf leaped at me, and I closed my eyes in resignation.

OOOOO

The shadow moves down the road through the park, sniffing and listening for the one that she seeks, the one that she has been asked to teach and must now save. There she is, behind the building with one of those abominations just like the ones that she had killed only a short time before. She took a step forward to rush to the daughter's rescue, knowing that she would never make it in time. She watches the wolf leap at her charge but stops in amazement and shock at the sight before her.

OOOOO

I closed my eyes, throwing out both arms instinctively to protect myself from the leaping wolf. It hit my body with all its weight and once more we went down in a tangled heap to the ground. We rolled around, my hands wrapped around the creature's throat digging into the soft fur when we came to a stop against an overturned table with me on top of the wolf. That's when I realized that it had stopped moving except for a few feeble shudders.

I heard a low whimper as I felt wetness pumping through my fingers. I slowly opened my eyes and then wished that I had left them closed. I watched as the last bit of blood slowly leaked through the hands that were embedded in the creature's fur. I released my grip and raised my hands away from the fur and blood and nearly fainted when I saw how they had changed.

My normally petite hands were now misshapen with long silver claws extending from bony fingers. Then I flexed my arms and felt the muscles move under my skin. I had always been well-built before from all the workouts that my mother made me do every day, but just the sight of the muscles that bulged from my arms almost made me swoon with fright. What the hell was going on here tonight?

Jumping up I watched as the wolf shifted back to Jason. Yeah, that Jason, the Jason that felt like 'my forever'. The one that I had been talking to and thinking that here I had found my one and only love in the first try, Jason. The Jason who now lay on the cement sidewalk naked with his throat ripped out and his blood pooling beneath him. I didn't know what was going on here, but whatever it was I was seriously losing my mind as I felt the world suddenly spin and all went black.

OOOOO

The shadow watched all that happened between the werewolf and the daughter and gave a small chuckle as the girl passed out after killing her foe. Looking around the dark night, trying to see if anyone had noticed this little ruckus in the park she moved slowly toward the two now lying on the ground and snickered. "Yeah, some warrior this one is going to make."

Drawing the silver blade once more from its sheath, she could feel the blade vibrate in anticipation of tasting the blood of a werewolf even though the foe on the ground was already dead. She approached carefully for she still carried the scars from one of these damn creatures that had been faking their death. Of course, they hadn't been faking long – once her sword dispatched the creature to the beyond. Still one must always be careful in dealing with these mongrels, as the tingle of old scars on her back warned. With a quick swish, the blade separated the head of the creature lying on the ground, once and for all assuring that this shifter would never hurt others again.

Sheathing the blooded but satisfied blade, she walked over to the other figure on the ground and bent down to make sure that the girl was still breathing. The small rise and fall of the girl's chest reassured her and she took a small breath of her own in relief. Now she just needed to get the daughter back to her own place and then she could discharge her duty to the mother who was now dead.

Slowly the diminutive shadow bends over and hitches the girl over her shoulders. Standing up the figure moves with a grace that belied the weight that she carried on her shoulders, and she heads out into the dark toward another part of the city.

OOOOO

I slowly opened my eyes and I rolled over in the warm comfortable bed that I was lying in. The early dawn's light shining through a crack in the heavy curtains showed that I was in some hotel room. I mean with all the moving my mother and I had done over the years, I was familiar with the layout of hotel rooms. Jerking up, I look around trying to figure out how I got here from the cold concrete I had been laying on when I passed out. While I had no idea how I had gotten in here, I had no wish to stay and find out either. I threw the blankets and sheets aside then I decided that maybe I was going to stay here a little longer after all since whoever had brought me here had taken all my clothes. I hastily covered myself back up with the sheet when I heard a small chuckle from one of the dark corners of the room. "Nice view there," a low voice whispered.

I tried to pierce the darkness of the room, but all I could catch was the outline of a small person sitting on a chair in the corner. "Who are you and why am I here?"

The silence from the corner spooked me a little and I clutched the sheets tighter to my body. Sitting up straighter on the bed, I put my back to the headboard. Another small chuckle issued from the darkness. "My name is Shane."

I looked at the shadow that just sat there then noticed the small lamp on the bedside table next to me. "You mind if I add a little light to this conversation?" I said reaching toward the lamp. Since there was no answer again I took that as an affirmative and flicked the switch, lighting up the room with a weak illumination.

I peered over toward the corner where the voice had issued from and gave a small chuckle of my own at the sight. A petite person sat there, cross-legged in a ratty green motel chair. She wore a black tee shirt with the sleeves cut off, black pants, and shiny black combat boots. But the weirdest thing of all was her hair. The hair had been cut all along the side of her head except for the vast amount that was spiked up so it stood up on her head like a shark fin. I looked around the room and didn't see any of my clothes and I was still wondering how and why I was here. "So, Shane was it? Could you tell me where my clothes are? And I'll just get out of your hair."

Shane frowned and as I watched her hair changed from black to red tinged. "Is there something so wrong with my hair that you want to leave this room?"

I held up one hand to ward off any misunderstandings, but when the sheet started to slip I grabbed it once more with a small squeak. "Oh no, nothing wrong at all, Shane. I just meant how about you get me some clothes and I'll just leave you to whatever it is you do here in your room."

The frown went away and she gave a small smile as her hair once more turned back to its original color. "Oh yes, I see what you mean now." Then the smile disappeared and was replaced once more with a serious look. "But I can't get your clothes because I burned them."

"BURNED THEM," I yelled then caught myself and continued in a calmer voice. "Shane, why did you burn my clothes? Now, what am I going to wear home?" Then it hit me that I was so going to be dead when I got home as I looked at the little light that shone through the split in the curtains.

The figure who sat in the chair just gave me a sad smile. "I burned your clothes because they were covered with shifter blood. Now if you are done with the hysterics, Ruby Red, I will go out and get you some new stuff while you get cleaned up."

Hysterics indeed, I thought, as I kept my calm this time while I glanced around the room seeing that there wasn't a thing for me to wear. And come to think about it, I did feel pretty sticky and grimy in some unusual places, not to say anything about all the aches and pains that I felt over my body. "Well okay, I guess a hot shower would feel good, but I want to be alone to take one, alright?"

Shane gave me a wide smile as she stood up and walked toward the door. "Oh you so would not fit into the Queen's court with an attitude like that, Ruby Red," she said as she opened the door and walked out into the hallway.

I heard a little click after she quietly closed it, and gathering the sheets around me I bounded out of the bed and tried the doorknob. Damn, I couldn't even turn the knob to open the door. I don't know what that little sneaky thing did, but whatever it was I guess I wasn't going anywhere even if I did have clothes to wear. I kicked the door in frustration, but of course, all that did was hurt my toes leaving me still frustrated, but now with a sore foot when I heard a small chuckle on the other side of the door then receding footsteps.

Then it hit me. The phone, no matter how much trouble I was going to get in, all I had to do was call my mother and she would come and get me. No matter where I went as I grew up, I knew that my mother could always find me. I tightened the sheet around me just in case Shane decided to make a surprise return to the room and walked over to the table by the bed. Nope, no phone there. Now if I was someone like her, where would I hide the phone? I tore through the room for ten minutes looking for the phone or even anything to tell me where I was but had no success.

I sat on the bed, tired and frustrated, looking over at the bathroom and thinking of the hot shower that awaited me when I gazed over at the window. Well, maybe I could open the window and yell out for someone to come and get me I wondered as I moved toward my salvation. I opened the drapes and looked at the window that was blacked out two-thirds of the way up. I figured that yeah maybe I could see out, but no one was going to see into the room.

I tried the window and sure enough, the thing wouldn't budge an inch, but turning I gave a sly smile as I spied the chair sitting next to the bathroom door. Walking over, I let the sheet fall to the floor knowing that I needed to be free of the cloth that surrounded me to get a good toss with my new battering ram. I would show that little pipsqueak that she was no match for the likes of me.

I moved back to the side of the window with the chair and hauling back I threw it with all my strength, turning away from the shower of glass that I figured could come back into the room. Unfortunately for me, the glass didn't break and all the chair did was bounce off the window then the wall and into my back, knocking me down to the floor.

I lay there under the chair, trying to catch my breath and thinking words that my mother would be shocked at if she could read my mind. Finally, I figured I wasn't going anywhere so I slowly crawled up from under from the chair and headed through the mess I had made in the room and toward the shower.

# THE HUNT

A large lone figure looks out the top floor of his office down at all those that walked by his building through the slow drizzle coming down in his city. He watches them as they scurry forward to visit the famous seaside market or the iconic tower from the World's Fair that marks the city landscape with its familiar shape. His building isn't the largest in the city, definitely not the prettiest, but from its interior, he controls this city and the surrounding states around it with ruthless abandon.

A quiet knock on the door brings him out of his meditation, he turns to see his assistant Joel enter the room. From the smell of fear rolling off his subordinate, he knows that all has not gone as planned once again. Just how long can that damn women keep hiding what is rightfully his? It was bad enough that she had made a fool of him when she had escaped into thin air, but to go so long dodging his men was unacceptable. Looking up, the smell from the one that entered his inner sanctum makes his nostrils flare in anticipation of the kill. Before he is overcome with the desire to slaughter, he takes a deep breath and steps back with a growl, "Well? What went wrong this time?"

The man before him looks down at sheets of paper clutched limply in his hand then back up at the one in front of him. "Marcus, the lady was killed, but . . ."

A long deep howl of satisfaction escapes from his throat, making his assistant jump several steps back. Marcus stands there, a huge smile of satisfaction and relief creeping across his face. He freezes at the next words that are whispered by the assistant, "But I was trying to tell you, we missed the girl."

"How could a slip of a girl get by the crew we sent, Joel? I mean she is only what fifteen, sixteen years old?" The quiet deadly whisper crosses the room making his smell of fear rise and assault the leader's nose once again.

The smaller man shrinks even more within himself as he glances down again at the papers that he holds. "Well sir, actually she is eighteen now. . ."

A quiet chuckle and then the leader steps back once more and leans against the desk behind him. "So she has hit the time of change, has she? Good, that is very good. Go on, there is more, isn't there? It seems that there is always more when it concerned that damn lady." So many times he had cursed the day he saw her, that is until the desire to once more control her takes over his body.

Joel glances down at the papers and looks up once more at the leader of the organization and into eyes that are impatient for him to finish. He shivers slightly, knowing that Marcus is the head of the organization through his ruthlessness killer instinct and is not known for his sparkling personality. "It also looks like she had help. One of 'them' wiped out the crew and is hiding her somewhere."

Slowly Marcus stands from the desk, his eyes now going a dark gold in color; his beast just roaming below the surface of his skin. In fact, as Joel watches, he can see the muscles below the skin ripple as though just waiting to take its true form once again. "That is not possible. They would have no use for a half-breed, especially one like her. Why would any of them help her? This is very puzzling. First, she brings my daughter into my territory after hiding her all these years and now another of these creatures shows up? It must be the power she processes, yes, that might be the reason that they interfere here."

"I'm sorry, sir, but no one survived to answer your question, but we . . ." the man's voice stops as the leader holds up his hand, palm out.

Slowly he walks over and looks down on his assistant, who by now is frozen in his fear as the rabbit is before the rabid wolf. "Here is what I want done. I want three crews to take that town apart, bit by bit until they find her and whoever is hiding her. Then I want her brought here to me along with the hide of her 'friend' so that I can hang it on my wall. Is that clear to you?"

"Sir, do you think that would be wise, I mean to hang the hide of a fae . . ."

Marcus doesn't say a word. He stands there in his inner sanctum, glaring at the one before him that would dare question his orders. Maybe it is time to change assistants again. Too bad. This one had been pretty good at keeping the everyday stuff from interfering with his life.

Marcus's overbearing power snaps his assistant out of his stupor. "Yes, sir. I will get on it right away. sir," the man says with a quick bow and turns to leave the room, grateful that he will live one more day to see the sunset. Not really knowing how close to dying he was, but he stops at the doorway of the office at the voice that whispers from behind him.

"Oh and Joel? Do not come back into this office without either my daughter or the hide of the one that is helping her." No answer is needed as the man once again gives a quick bow and shuts the door behind him.

Marcus looks at the closed door and once more wanders over to the window. There is so much to think about. First, that damn woman takes his only heir, hell, the only female of their kind with these kinds of powers, even if she is a half-breed, and then returns right under his nose with her. Maybe this isn't just about his daughter. Maybe the women and her kind are trying, once more, to take his land away from him. The reason doesn't matter, though. No matter what, he needs to have this girl to teach her the right way to rule the humans and Supers that his wolves look down on with contempt. And who knows, if the rumors are true about the powers that the girl processes, with her he could rule this whole land from coast to coast.

As these thoughts percolate in Marcus's mind, he paces back and forth in front of the window, reluctantly thinking that maybe it is time that he brings in the other shifter families to help with this problem, but that, he knows, would be a show of weakness on his part and something that one in his position can never do. No, for right now he would make quiet inquiries and hope that the teams sent out from here will take care of the problem in the right way. No reason, right now, to tip his hand to the other families that rule this country. No, for now, they would solve this problem within the organization.

Stepping over to the desk, he smiles as he thinks of the perfect person to handle the inquiries he will need. He is a sneaky little rat, but right now he is the one that can get the job done. With that decided, he pushes the button on the speaker box on his desk. "Yess ssir?" Joel's voice stammers from the box.

He shakes his head at the frightened tone of Joel's voice. Maybe it is time for a new assistant he thinks once more, smiling at thought of the hunting and killing of another shifter which is usually more of a challenge than the humans they usually have. He shakes his head to clear these thoughts, then growls, "Tell Mack I want to see him now."

"Yes, sir, right away si . . ."

He flips off the button and walks back to the window to look down on those beneath him once more. There are more important things that need to be taken care of today than pleasures of the kill, the taste of blood. With that thought, Marcus moves back to his desk and the paperwork that beckons with a snarl of impatience. That's when his personal phone rings, looking down he sees his mate's number. With a grimace of frustration and anger, he tosses his phone into the garbage and whispers, "Another thorn in my side that needs to be taken care of."

OOOOO

Standing in the shower, feeling the heat of the water wash all the grime off of me and soothe my aching body my mind drifts. I think back to all the work that my mother had me do in the gym. Lifting weights, gymnastics, martial arts, and I wonder deep down how much of all that effort saved my life last night. It seemed that ever since I could walk, my mother had had a training area set up in our house and there always seemed to be someone coming over to teach me how to – well, how to kill, to put it bluntly.

As I thought back over the years and the different instructors I had a memory of someone that looked just like Shane. But that couldn't be right because as I thought of that time I remembered that I was probably about five years old, and Shane looked no older than I was now, well actually Shane looked no older than ten with her short stature and petite size. So, of course, it couldn't have been her. I guess after all that had happened to me last night I was maybe slightly losing my grip on reality.

I moved slowly in the shower, still feeling the bumps and bruises of last night as the water started to turn cold. Turning off the faucet, I stepped out of the shower and grabbed the towel that was on a rack over the toilet. Did I say towel? I think I have seen wash cloths bigger than what I held in my hand, but it was the only thing in the room that I had to dry off with until Shane brought me some clothes.

I spent several minutes taking care of other bathroom necessities when the smell of hot food wafted under the bathroom door. Well, I guess that meant that my captor (rescuer?) was back with something to eat and, hopefully, something to wear.

Opening the door, I stepped out of the bathroom wearing that small piece of cloth some would call a towel, and stopped as I looked around the room in shock. I had trashed it not even a half hour ago and now everything was back in its place. There sat Shane in the chair that I had broken when I threw it at the window. "What the hell, how did you do that?" I said knowing that whatever Shane was, she wasn't human.

"Do what?"

I took a deep breath and looked around the room once more. "The room? How did you clean up the mess and repair the chair like that?"

Shane sat there quietly on the chair, cross-legged, looking at me with a sly smile. "Are you feeling better now, Ruby Red, after your little temper tantrum?" she asked, ignoring my question.

I just sighed and filed whatever she did with the other weird stuff that had happened to me last night and this morning. "Yeah, I feel better now. I smell food, but did you get me clothes?"

Shane glanced past me into the bathroom and nodded her head. "Why, of course, I did they are sitting right there on the toilet seat. Were you planning on running around the room all day in that itty bitty piece of cloth or were you going to get dressed?" she asked in a snarky voice.

I turned back and looked into the bathroom as I was starting to tell this weird person that there were no clothes in there but the words never left me mouth as I spied the small pile of clothes that now sat on the closed toilet lid that I had only seconds ago used.

I whipped around and saw another sly smile on Shane's face, "How . . ." but I stopped what I was going to ask, took two steps back into the bathroom and slammed the door and clicked the door lock on that mocking face. Not that I really thought the lock would keep that person out of the room if Shane had wanted to come in. I sat down on the edge of the tub as I felt myself start to go faint. I wasn't sure what was going on here, but I knew one thing and that was that I needed to get away from this strange person and her strange little ways.

I figured the first thing I had to do was to get dressed and then figure out a way to either get out of this room or to let my mother know where I was. In fact, I was pretty surprised that my mother wasn't already trying to track me down right now, knowing her. Something was wrong. I could feel it in my bones. My mother never left me out of her sight for this long in the entire time I had been old enough to notice such things.

So with that thought, I grabbed the clothes that were on the toilet and started to get dressed. I must admit I wasn't surprised at the choices that Shane had chosen for my outfit. I had a matching set of black jeans, and black tee-shirt, but this one with sleeves, thank god, but instead of combat boots, I saw that she had gotten me a pair of black athletic shoes. Her color sense or lack thereof really sucked, but Shane was pretty good at guessing sizes, as everything fit me perfectly.

Looking at myself in the mirror, I was glad of one thing and that was that the shirt that she had gotten me was a little larger than I usually wear since Shane seemed to have forgotten about a bra and panties for me. With what I was wearing it was no big deal, but as with girls built as I was, it could get a little embarrassing in a tight shirt showing off more then I wanted everyone to see.

Opening the door and walking out into the room once

again, I found that Shane was now sitting cross-legged on the bed and the only chair in the room was pulled up to the small round table holding the hot steaming food that she had brought back from wherever she had gone before. Walking over to the table, I purposely ignored Shane and sat down and started to gobble down the food since all of a sudden I had this burning desire to eat as my stomach rumbled in protest at being empty for so long and from the aroma of the food that filled the room.

It was silent in the room for a few minutes except for the sounds of my fork hitting the plate until Shane whispered, "I would have figured that your mother taught you better than this, Ruby Red."

"Better then what?" I asked with the fork stopped halfway between my mouth and the plate.

That irritating smile once more appeared on Shane's face. "Well, how do you know that I haven't put something in it to make you sleep so that I could have my wicked way with you or even worse, I might have poisoned that food?"

I slowly lowered the fork as I looked down at my nearly empty plate, glancing back and forth between Shane and the remaining food. She was right, though, my mother had taught me that if I was ever taken that one thing an enemy could do was put drugs or worse in the food. Here I always thought it was just the old girl being paranoid. "Oh man," was all I could get out in a quiet whisper as the last bite of food I had taken hit my stomach. Was that a little bit of dizziness coming on?

Shane sat there for a few seconds then burst out laughing, her hair turning a bright blue. It was one of those laughs from deep down where you throw your head back and it bounces off the walls and ceiling. Since I was the butt of that laugh I wasn't too thrilled with it and looked down at my plate once more when Shane stopped laughing and whispered, "JK".

Yeah right, I thought, as I set the fork down on the plate and made to stand up from the table suddenly not at all hungry any more. I figured that if I could make it to the bathroom in a few seconds I could rid myself of anything still in my stomach.

Before I could get up, I blinked and Shane was standing next to me dipping her hands into my food and taking a bite from what she held. "See its good, no drugs or poison," she said through a full mouth.

I must have blinked again because Shane was now sitting cross-legged on the bed, this time eating what she had pilfered off of my plate. I sat there for a couple of more seconds before my stomach urged me to fill it again with a low rumble of protest since I had stopped eating. So I picked up the fork and started back in on the food that was sitting in front of me ignoring the person that was sitting on the bed, especially since her eating habits would have given my mother fits if she had been in the room with us. As that thought crossed my mind, I wondered once more just where my mother was and why she wasn't here rescuing me from the clutches of this insane person. As I took the last forkful, Shane smiled at me once again. "Of course, I could be used to any sleepy potion or poison I put into your food."

OOOOO

Sitting back in my chair, now fed I looked at her smile and just ignored her words. But I was still curious about what was going on and who this Shane character really was. I gave my 'roommate' a better once over and noticed that I was wrong before about one thing and that the one sitting before me may have been small in stature, but Shane was well muscled for one of her size.

In fact, as I looked more closely, except for the weird mood shifting hairdo Shane reminded me of a picture of a pint-sized ninja I had once seen. The silence in the room finally got to me and I broke it figuring that now was the time to get some answers. "Okay, Shane, just who are you? And no bull from you, just answer the question."

Shane sat there for several seconds and then her hair turned a light blue with the smile that lit up her face. "Just answer the question or what, Ruby Red?"

Okay, she had me there as I glanced at the pair of swords that still hung across her back. Well then let's just try tact, I thought. "Okay then, plea. . ."

Shane jumped off the bed toward me, her hair turning

bright red holding both hands in front of her as though to ward off my words and yelled, "NO, DON'T SAY THAT WORD TO ME, RUBY RED."

I stopped in mid-sentence and sat back in my seat, a little frightened at her reaction to saying a simple little word like 'please'. I let the quiet in the room settle over us as Shane stood there, her chest heaving from the outburst that it had just produced. After a minute, Shane seemed to calm down somewhat and once more crawled up on the bed and sat cross-legged in the same spot as she had before.

"Your mother was surely lacking if she did not teach you not to say that word to one such as I, Ruby Red," Shane whispered and then bowed her head looking down at the bedspread that held the remnants of her breakfast.

I took a deep breath and figured to start over when Shane looked up at me and whispered, "I am a minor fae, Ruby Red, but even still with one as me you never ever say 'please' or 'thanks' or you will own a favor to that fae, and there are some fae you do not want to owe favors to."

"Okay and that would be bad . . ." I stopped and then it hit me just what she had said. "Shane you mean you are a fae? You mean like a fairy? Sort of like Tinker Bell and all that kind of stuff fae? Is what you're telling me?"

Shane's hair that had been fading to black again but suddenly turned a brilliant shade of red and she started to float about a foot off the bed. I glanced at her eyes then looked away as I saw then go a deep pure dark blue. I mean there was no other color there at all just the dark blue filling those eyes, giving the illusion of the water at the bottom of a deep cold well. A low growl issued from the floating person before me. "Do not ever mistake me for some cartoon character, Ruby Red, or you would regret it for the remainder of your very short young life."

I stood up from the chair, knocking it back down onto the floor my anger flaring to the point that I could feel the hairs rise up on my arms and the back of my neck. I glanced down at my hands and saw that once more my fingers had extended, my nails had turned into the claws of some animal. Looking closer, though, I could see that the claws had a dark sheen the color of iron rather than the bright silver that they had been last night.

We stayed like that for several minutes, Shane floating in the air while I crouched by the table waiting to see what she would do next. With a small laugh, the fae extended her legs down so that they were now touching the bed while her hair and eyes slowly returned to their natural color. "Well, it's nice to see that you aren't totally helpless, Ruby Red. Now, why don't you pick up that chair and have a seat and I'll explain how the real world works for those of our kind."

# THE REAL WORLD

Mack sat perfectly still outside the chairman's inner sanctum as the other shifters moved around him, his usual nervous energy on hold around such creatures as these. He knew that he was only tolerated for his usefulness and what information he could bring Marcus, the leader of this organization. If not for his ability in this area, one such as he would soon fall prey to those that were at the top of the food chain since rats definitely were not at the top of this food chain.

With a sneer and a look of loathing, the man that sat at the desk put down the phone and stood up and looked at Mack. "Marcus will see you now." With those words, the wolf turned his back and walked toward the double doors, opening them without looking to see if the rat was following.

Mack jumped up from his chair and hurried after the assistant; following him into the office and figuring that it was probably a fifty-fifty chance that he wouldn't come out of there alive. He stopped a few feet in and gave a nervous little twitch when he heard the doors quietly being closed behind him. He stood silently waiting for the man that sat behind the desk to acknowledge his presence.

Marcus sat there knowing the second that the lowly creature before him had entered his space, but enjoying the discomfort and smell of fear that emitted from one such as him. Looking up from his papers, he slowly rose from his seat and scowled. "I have a job for you, rat."

Mack moved up to the desk, his head bowed and his eyes locked onto the ground before him. He knew that convincing Marcus that his subservient attitude was genuine would be the only way he would walk out of this room alive. "Yes sir, of course, anything that you want or that I can . . ."

The wolf leaped across the desk, his large right hand closing across Mack's throat and cutting off his remarks in mid-sentence. Slowly raising the smaller man up into the air, a sly smile appeared on Marcus's face as Mack's legs kicked and the small face started to turn blue. "Shut up and listen to me, rat, if you know what is good for you." With that, the big man dropped the smaller one onto the floor where he lay gasping and fighting to bring air into his lungs.

In the silence of the office, Mack wonders, as he lies on the floor if a fifty-fifty chance of walking out of this room was being too generous. He knows that his life now hangs in the balance; it's in the hands of the one standing before him and he huddles down trying to make himself look as harmless as he can.

Marcus stands there fighting the urge to destroy this creature on the floor but knows that he needs him for jobs that only this rat can accomplish. He thinks that maybe it is time to take off from this work and enjoy a hunt since it seems harder and harder to still the killing instinct within him. "I want you to find out why the fae is in my territory, rat."

Mack looks up in surprise and then quickly back down at the floor. "The fae, sir? Are you sure? I mean I have heard nothing about fae in Seattle," he mumbles then ducks down at the expected blow that never comes from questioning the leader of the organization.

A low growl sounds above him then quiet once more descends in the office. "You are so lucky, rat, that I need you. Now get out of my office and find out all you can about any fae that are in my territory. All of my territory – got me, rat?"

A swift kick from Marcus into the middle of the shifter's body helps get Mack moving toward the door. Rolling with the kick and then going to his hands and knees, Mack moves as fast as he can toward the only way out of the room. Reaching up, he opens one of the doors just wide enough to slip out into the outer office and slams it behind him.

Resting against the door for a few seconds, he spies the

looks that the other shifters in the room throw him – looks of disgust and loathing for his kind. Keeping a bland look pasted on his face hiding his hatred of those around him he thinks even when I'm needed I'm still treated like scum by these creatures. Well, one day they will pay for their arrogance. He gets to his feet and walks by the sneers and small chuckles keeping his eyes glued to the ground.

As he walks out of the outer office and down the hall, hugging the walls he thinks how interesting it would be if the fae were trying to move on the organization. That hadn't happened in a long time, but, of course, the fae had a long memory. Maybe this was about the rumors of a missing princess from the major house years ago that circulated around here. He smiles at the thought that he was one of the first to start those rumors and is still surprised to this day that the shifters never figured that one out. Well, whatever the reason, if the fae were making a move on this territory he needed to find out for sure. Not so much for the ones in this building as for the lower creatures and shifters like him that these dogs ruled.

OOOOO

I watched as Shane leisurely sat back down on the bed and then leaned back on her elbows. I was reluctant to relax my guard, remembering just how fast that fae could move, but it was getting tiring crouching here waiting for any movement from the person in front of me.

Shane cocked an eyebrow at me and chuckled. "You going

to stand there like that all day or you going to relax, sit down, and listen to what I have to say?"

A growl escaped from my throat, a sound that I had never heard from myself and I jumped a little in surprise from the noise. Standing up from my crouch, I could feel the anger leaving me, but there was a certain wariness that wouldn't go away. "Okay, I'll listen to what you say as long as afterward you let me go back home."

Shane sat up on the bed in a flash and once more I was crouching next to the table, my newfound claws extended toward the fae. "Sorry, sorry, it's just that is something else we need to discuss when the time comes. Now sit down and I promise that I will answer any questions you have after I have my say, okay?"

I relaxed and then reached back for the chair on the floor nodding my head at Shane. Sitting down, once I got the chair positioned right, I watched as the fae took a deep breath and then slowly leaned back onto her elbows once again. I could feel the hairs on my arms and neck loosen up and glanced down at my hands that were now minus the claws that I had had only seconds ago. I looked up from my hands once more at Shane and asked my first question. "Don't take this wrong, but, you are a girl right?"

I could see just the palest pink then red highlight Shane's hair before it went dark black once more with her laughter. "Don't sweat it, Ruby Red, you're safe with me – I'm a female fae."

Looking at her small but well-built body, I could see that I was right – she was more wiry and muscled than anything and that even without the swords mounted across her back I would probably not like to meet her in a dark alley. "Okay just curious what was with that little comment you made before when I had only a sheet, I just . . ."

Shane gave another laugh and gave me a quick once over. "Sorry about that, I forgot that humans in this world, not that you are human, but that was how your mother raised you, are sensitive about sex and being naked around others. But just to let you know I'm attracted to other women."

"Oh, I see. Well just to let you know, I mean, I don't, you know, swing that way."

Shane got a puzzled look on her face. "Swing, you're not swinging anywhere, you're just sitting."

I shook my head and sighed. "I mean I like boys. Never mind about that. What did you mean before that I'm not human?"

Shane gave me this stare, her right eyebrow cocked giving me a 'like really' look and then I thought back to what had happened to my hands with the claws, with the increased muscle mass, and with the temper. Well okay so maybe the temper wasn't something so new after all. "Okay, yeah, so I may not be quite all human. Is what you're telling me?"

Shane snickered. "Oh, Ruby Red you aren't even a little human."

Now I was starting to get pissed at her attitude. "Okay well then tell me exactly what I am if not human, smart ass."

I tensed up a little as Shane sat up on the bed, and then relaxed at her smile. "Okay let me tell you about the real world, child. You see there are humans and then there are the Supernaturals for want of a better word."

"Supernaturals, yeah right. Nice nickname there, Shane."

Shane blustered a little bit with her hair once more tingeing red then she settled down with a small laugh of her own. "Don't try me, Ruby Red. But hey, it's the humans that came up with that name, not us. Now you want me to finish or not?"

"Yeah, sorry, go on."

"Alright then. Now where was I? Oh yeah, the world is divided into territories with the fae living in Europe and the areas around it for the most part with minor creatures occupying smaller parts of the continent. Most of this side of the world is the territory of the shapeshifters with a small band of vamps living down south. Asia is a mix of shifters and other creatures such as Asian dragons with a few other things that go bump in the night thrown into the mix."

I looked at the girl sitting on the bed and thought for a second that I really needed to get to a phone and call the loony bin on this chick then I reflected back on all that had happened last night and today and decided that maybe I needed to make a reservation for the two of us. "Okay then so what you are telling me is that Jason, the boy I was with last night, was a werewolf or shifter as you called them and that I'm what, one of these shifters too because I get a little muscled and have claws?"

Shane was nodding her head as I asked my question and a large smile spread across her face. I felt like I was five years old again and ready to get a gold star for answering my teacher's question. "Right in one, Ruby Red, except that you are not quite all werewolf where Jason was.

"Okay say I believe you. I mean it's a little hard not to after watching the small changes that happened to me, I guess, but I didn't change all the way into a wolf like Jason for one thing. And how come nobody really believes in the fae, vamps, and werewolves and all that. I mean yeah we make up stories and movies, but deep down no one really thinks that these creatures are real."

The smile disappeared off of Shane's face. "Oh, we are real alright, Ruby Red, and the humans that are in charge, and a few others know that we are real. As for you not changing into a full werewolf, well that day is coming."

"And these people don't say anything because why?" I asked completing ignoring the statement about my day of change was going to come. For some reason deep down I knew that she was right and right then didn't want to think about it too much.

The smile returned as Shane answered. "Oh, that's easy.

They don't say anything because we, for the most part, control them is why and the ones that we don't control are labeled as nut cases and such."

"Oh," was all I could get out at the thought of creatures of our nightmares controlling humans. I know Shane said I wasn't human, but just because my father was some kind of creature didn't make me all wolf. I mean there was no way that my mother was a werewolf; you would have thought I'd know about her going furry once a month, right? Once again the image of changing into a huge canine like Jason had flashed across my mind and I shook my head to rid it of that picture.

I sat there thinking over what the fae had told me when another little problem popped into my head. "Shane, if the fae live in Europe then what are you doing here in Washington State? I mean won't that tick off some shifter? I mean aren't you kind of invading their territory?"

The smile once again dropped from her face like a lead balloon. Shane stood up and started to pace back and forth in the small area between the bed and the outside door of the room. She was quiet for a few minutes and I let her pace and dig out whatever demon she seemed to be fighting within herself when she stopped and turned to face me. "I came here to protect a fae princess and her daughter, Ruby Red, but I failed one and now I need to see that the other is safe and brought back home before her father finds her."

"Oh, well I'm sorry that I got in the way . . ." I stopped and really looked at Shane as she shook her head from side to side then it hit me. "My mother is the fae princess you are talking about and I'm the daughter, aren't I?"

"Yes, Ruby Red, you are that daughter."

I glanced down at the floor then l jerked my head back to look at Shane once more. "Wait! You said you failed to protect my mother, you mean . . ."

With a trace of sadness, her voice, in a whisper I could barely hear, answered, "Your mother died last night fighting men from your father's organization."

I jumped up from the chair I had been sitting on; it bounced off the table and hit the floor, as I headed toward the door of the room. "Oh hell no, you're mistaken nothing could kill my mother."

I reached the door in three steps where Shane now stood, looking at me with eyes so full of pity that I just wanted to mash that look right off of her face. "You either move or I move you. Right now I could not care which of those choices you make, fae," I said as I felt the hairs on my arms and neck ruffle in the heat of anger and the claws grow in my clenched fists so that they dug into the soft flesh of my hands. I glanced down and saw the muscles rippling under the flesh of my arms. Oh yeah, I'm definitely not human.

Shane slowly moved to the side of the small entranceway and I reached for the door as she laid her smaller hand on my arm. "It isn't safe out there for you, Ruby Red. I have killed the ones that took your mother from you, but by now this town will be crawling with more dogs looking for you."

I stopped and slowly breathed in and out for a few seconds as I felt the hairs and claws retreat from the calmness that I forced on myself. I knew that I couldn't walk around Bellingham looking like a half-wild creature in the middle of the day, but I needed to find out for sure that Shane was telling the truth about my mother. "I'm going, and I really don't give a damn about anyone my father sends after me."

"Fine, then I will go with you Ruby Red and you will see that I am telling you the truth."

I glanced at her and then thought of venturing out where creatures like Jason, or maybe worse, were hunting me or at least they were according to the fae standing before me. As I looked at the two swords slung across her back, I thought that I may be stubborn, but I wasn't stupid so I nodded my head at her suggestion. "Alright, you can come with me but once I prove you wrong you leave me alone, you hear me?"

Shane said, "Of course." Managing a little bow within the confined area we were in. I should have known right there that she wasn't telling the truth as she gave in to my demands too easily. We walked out the door of the room and into an unknown future.

# ENFORCERS

The wolves were all in human form since it wouldn't do to scare the locals, not that he really cared what humans thought, but rules were rules after all. And even enforcers had to follow the rules set by the Council of Shifters. Joseph was the head enforcer for the organization and figured that this kind of job was beneath his status. But when orders were issued from Marcus himself even he moved without question. Now if only he could clear up this little mess that had been plaguing the organization for all these years and get back down to Seattle. He liked the big city where if a stray human or two went missing nobody would care. With all the work he had been putting in lately, he figured that he deserved a modest treat after this little job was done.

The three vehicles arrived in this small college town in a caravan. Two of them, each with four specialists inside, were even now scouring the town for any clue as to the whereabouts of the leader's daughter and the rumored fae that was with her. He and his crew were at the scene of what looked like the aftermath of a small battle. Getting out of the black SUV, he and his men walked over to the taped-off area where a lone cop was watching their approach.

One of the shifters with Joseph sniffed the air and growled, "Human," his voice dripping with disdain and a little bit of hunger.

Joseph glanced to the side and quietly snarled at his companion who suddenly lost his bravado and took several steps back to blend in with the other two shifters in the group. Joseph reached into his jacket pocket and took out special I.D. that all wolf shifters carried in this territory and flashed it at the young policeman. "Hello Officer . . . Wilkins is it?" Joseph said as he glanced at the officer's name tag. "We need to talk to whoever is in charge here."

The young rookie who was sitting out on the perimeter of his first crime scene looked first at the credentials that were being waved in his face and then at the trio behind them. "That would be Detective Johnson, sir," the officer said with a yawn.

Wilkins had never seen these kinds of badges before, but with all the new type of Feds that were running around he figured that they were just someone else that the higher ups needed to deal with, after a few seconds of hesitation the officer said, "Oh right sir, just let me call him," as he reached for his radio and moved off a few steps.

A barely audible growl escaped Joseph's lips. "Humans." Causing two of the men to chuckle as the third who had made the same remark earlier looked on in resentment.

Joseph started to turn and admonish the sulking member of his crew when he noticed Officer Wilkins walking back up to the tape, stop and salute him. "Sir, Detective Johnson will be right here."

Joseph nodded, arms crossed across his chest, standing silently waiting for the detective to make his appearance. The officer once more took in the four towering men and then turned his back on them to watch the crime scene crew do their job. Something in his subconscious clicked about the four behind him; the shadows that he and Michael had been watching last night -- these men were shifters just like the ones outside the girl's house. Michael would need to know about these new threats, besides the news of the aftermath seen in this little war zone that had happened in the middle of their town.

After a few seconds of dwelling on these thoughts, he felt four pairs of eyes focus on the back of his neck, causing a feeling of wariness to shiver up and down his spine. Damn, did these monsters know that he was part of the underground that fought creatures as these? With no conscious thought, he slowly brought his hand up to the side of his holster when he heard several low growls sound behind him. He started to turn to the perceived danger when he heard a voice of authority sound from in front of him. "WILKINS, what the hell do you think you're doing?"

Officer Wilkins started and heard low laughs sound behind him as he turned fully to face another large statured man that was marching up from the crime scene. "Nothing Detective Johnson, I was just . . ."

The detective stopped inches from the rookie's face, giving him a once over. This was the look everyone in the department recognized as meaning that they were on the detective's shithouse list. The detective quickly glanced over to the four men, before he once more turned his full attention to the person in front of him. "Rookie, I know you were not going to pull a weapon on these fine Feds now, were you?"

Wilkins straightened his back in defiance, but then just as fast withered under his superior's fierce look. "No sir?" he whispered back.

"That's good to know, rookie. Now get down to the crime scene and make yourself useful, if you think you can." With a nod and another quick glance behind him, Wilkins headed off toward where the main activity was going on around the destroyed bank and the surrounding streets.

As the officer walked away from the danger behind him, he figured that he really needed to get hold of Michael and let him know what was going on out here. Then with another yawn and a shake of his head, the officer glanced back at the group behind him and gave a little shudder at the thought of more of these creatures invading his hometown.

Detective Johnson stepped over to the tape, giving the

leader before him a nod of deference, but ignoring the other three men in the group gathered around them. "What are you here for?" he growled the question at Joseph in a small show of dominance, figuring all this was his part of the territory and he could handle things perfectly well all on his own.

Joseph ignored the implied challenge, knowing that there is more at stake here than some little turf squabble. "Was it fae that did this to the crews?" he asked, nodding at the wrecked vehicles and covered bodies that littered the small town streets.

The detective took in a deep breath, acknowledging that fighting the enforcer before him over turf would be a quick way to die right now and glanced back at the carnage down the street and then back at the four men. "That's what it smells like, but tell them down south that I have this handled. I'll get . . ."

A large hand moved in a blur, gripping the throat of the detective and cutting off his words as Joseph leaned closer and hissed, "I think you have handled this just enough. The man down south has sent us here to take care of the problem now, and if you want to live through this mess you will shut up and let us do our job. Do you understand, Detective?"

With a little push, Joseph shoved him away and then watched as the detective nodded. "Good then we will be on our way." And with that, he and the three men around him turned and walked back to their vehicle.

Finally sitting in the big SUV, they watched the detective walk back to the crime scene. Joseph turned to the biggest of three other men. "When this is over, get rid of him." The man smiled and nodded at the command he understood the best.

OOOOO

Walking along the streets of Bellingham toward my house, I was amazed after awhile that the pint-sized ninja walking beside me wasn't garnering any attention at all from the people either on the sidewalk or the ones that zipped by us on the streets in their vehicles. I mean come on, it isn't every day that someone walks down the street looking like a two-sword carrying bad ass in this town. We were almost to the road that leads to my house and as I glanced over every once and awhile at Shane, I could see a small sly smile play across her face at my confused looks, and finally I couldn't hold it back anymore. "Okay, how come no one is reacting to your weapons?"

"Glamour," was all I got out of her as she strolled down the sidewalk next to me.

I stopped for a second and then quickened my pace so that I was now once again walking beside her. "What are you talking about?"

Shane was shaking her head with some irritation. "Didn't your mother teach you anything about her people?"

"Well now that you put it that way, I guess not. So tell me what I need . . ."

I never got to finish my sentence for Shane had come to a sudden halt and had grabbed hold of my arm and was forcefully pulling me toward the trees nearby, a look of concern on her face. I tried to stop my movement to the tree line, but for being a small little package this girl was super strong. "Hey, what's up? Stop that," I tried to protest as we finally ducked into the trees.

"Hush, they'll hear you."

"Who will hear me? Why are we hiding when my house is just up the road here?"

Shane raised an eyebrow at me once I finished talking and pointed down the street at a police car that sat about half a mile away and the two cops that stood outside it. I watched it for a second then stood up straighter as the faint smell of smoke floated down on the breeze from where my home was. I tried to shake my arm loose from the steel grip that encircled it but was pulled deeper into the trees as a large black SUV went storming past our hiding place.

Shane kneeled down next to me where I had landed on my butt from our struggles and gave the SUV a quick glance before turning back to me. "Now listen Ruby Red and listen well if you want to live out the day. That vehicle that just passed us is full of your father's men. They will kill me and take you away to a place where you may not survive, or at least that is their plan. So you either do as I say or I leave you to fend for yourself."

I looked up at Shane's eyes and saw that if need be she would walk away from me with no hesitation and that thought scared me more than any of the other things that had happened to me the last couple of hours. I shook her hand off of my arm and stood up and glanced over at the two vehicles up the road and then back at Shane. "Alright, I'll follow you and do what you tell me to. I just want to go home and see my mother."

Shane nodded her head at me, a sad frown crossing her face as I caught just the slightest whiff of smoke on the air once more and I had this sinking feeling in the pit of my stomach that my wish for seeing my mother once again would not go as planned. "Okay then, follow me Ruby Red and quietly."

As we started deeper into the woods, I glanced back once more at the street and saw that the black SUV had disappeared and only the cop car was now in the middle of the road again. Since the SUV hadn't come back down the road, I figured that whoever was in it was now headed toward the same place that Shane and I were.

OOOOO

After another ten minutes of walking through the trees, I remembered why I was not one of those outdoorsy type girls as I tripped over the hundredth branch that jumped out from the ground and wrapped itself around my legs. Shane stopped with a quiet huff of impatience and for just as many times she looked at me and snorted in annoyance and shook her head. "What?" I whispered. "I can't help it."

Now the look of annoyance turned to anger as she slapped her finger to her mouth shushing me and then threw a glance at where the road should be. She quietly, of course, moved over to me and helped me up from the ground and put her mouth close to my ear whispering, "There are werewolves about, they can hear an ant burp from a mile away. So how about you watch where you're walking before you get us killed."

I nodded, eyes wide, and stood as I watched the silent little fae in front of me turn and once more move off in the direction of my house. As we got closer, the smell of smoke and something else, something like the smell of burnt meat started to get stronger and permeate the air around us. With each step forward, my heart sank further down into my stomach at the thought of what awaited us once we reached home.

We moved forward for about another five minutes until I recognized the back fence of our yard, but couldn't see any of my house beyond it. What I did see was the yellow crime scene tape that fluttered in the air just beyond the fence. Now all I could smell was the stink of old smoke and ashes from a fire that had been recently doused. I stood there stunned at the thought that my house was gone when the thought crossed my mind that that didn't mean that my mother had been in the house at the time of the fire. Then that other smell hit me and I knew that yeah my mother was gone and I slowly sank down to my knees, burying my face in my hands with a quiet sob.

OOOOO

I don't know how long I kneeled like that, but I felt Shane drop next to me and put her hand on my shoulder as the thought that I would never see my mother's face again seeped into my very soul. After what seemed like forever, but was only seconds later I'm sure I heard the snap of a branch behind me and I felt Shane's reassuring presence gone from my side.

As my mind processed the sounds of a struggle behind me, I scurried to my feet and turned as I watched a man's head separate from his body, bounce off of a tree and land near my feet. As I looked down, his eyes blinked once before they turned blank with death. I caught the fleeting impression of three figures having a sword fight in the woods when my attention was diverted by the pair of strong arms that encircled my waist, trapping my arms to the side of my body. "HEY, what the hel . . . "

"Now, now is that any way for a little girl to talk?" a low gravelly voice growled in my ear.

"I'll show you what kind of little girl I am," I said as I lifted my legs into the air and then I stomped down on the man's instep. The howl of pain and the loud snap of bone were a comfort to my ears and as he released his hold on me, I took one step back, planted my right foot and delivered a side kick into the center mass of my antagonist.

As my foot connected, I heard some more cracks as his ribs caved in from my kick. Damn it was nice to have this power rush when I was mad, bending the figure over and bringing him down to his knees. I took one step forward and brought my elbow down on the back of the man's exposed neck and watched his body hit the ground, his head cocked at this odd angle with some satisfaction. And the fae thought I couldn't take care of myself, well I showed her.

I felt a wave of nausea as the thought of what I had just done washed over me, when I heard a small cough behind me. I turned and crouched, looking for another enemy and feeling like I could take on the world when I saw Shane standing there, a small smile creasing her face. "Not bad, Ruby Red. Just one thing to remember," she said as she took a step forward. With a backhanded swipe, she swung her blade just past my face and through the neck of the man standing behind me – the one whose neck I had just broken two seconds ago. "You have to cut a werewolf's head off from their body to make sure that they are really dead."

As I turned, I watched the man's head go one way and his body drop back down onto the forest floor. I turned back to Shane and smiled as I looked over at the three decapitated bodies behind her. "Yeah I'll try and remember that, Shane."

The fae nodded and then walking over to the body, bending down she started to go through the man's pockets.

"Shane, are you looking for anything in particular?"

"Yes this, Ruby Red," she said as she stood up with the man's wallet. I watched as she rifled through it, taking out what cash was in it and an I.D. that she looked at for a few seconds. With a minute grunt, she walked over and handed me the card that she held in her hand. "Well, that answers that question."

I glanced at the Seattle driver's license then back at Shane, puzzled by the answer of a question I didn't even know. "Okay I'll bite, what answer did you get from his driver license?"

Shane shook her head and moved over to the other three men that littered the back area of what, just yesterday, was the house that my mother and I lived in. I stomped over to where she was bending over one of the other bodies making another search and then coming up with another wallet. I watched her as she once more looked at the driver's license, tossed it and then took some cash out of it.

Watching her stand up and add that money to the other bills she had gathered, I glanced around the woods and then back at her. "You know that it isn't right to take stuff from the dead, and just what answer are these guys giving us?"

Shane started over to the next body and then stopped and looked at me for a few seconds before answering my questions. "One, Ruby Red, is that it is right for me to take the spoils of war. Two is that the answer is that these creatures belong to your father since they are from Seattle."

I stood there as she turned from me and went to despoil the next body that lay at her feet. "Well just because these guys are from Seattle doesn't mean they are from my father, does it?"

Shane was quiet until she stood up from her self-imposed chore and then once again looked at me. "Ruby Red, let me set you straight on one thing. Your father rules everything from the Canadian border down to the California border. His territory also extends east to the Dakotas. So yes, if there are werewolves in his territory – which these are – then these are his men because no other wolves would live long enough to get this deep into his land if they aren't part of his organization."

I processed it all in and then watched as Shane walked over to the last body on the ground. "Okay, but I still don't think it is right that you take their money, Shane."

Shane just laughed; a sound that came from deep within her but held no humor. When she finished, she looked up at me her hair turning that deep shade of red while her eyes went to that scary all deep, dark blue look. "Believe me, Ruby Red, I have seen worse done on the battlefield to the dead than taking a few dollars from their body. Besides, we will need the money to survive." As I looked deep into those eyes, they had the look of a hundred years of misery written within them. I couldn't bear that look and broke eye contact first and stared down at the ground.

The fae then stood up and walked away from the bodies and headed deeper into the woods. "Where are we going, Shane?" I said as I glanced up at her departing back.

The fae stopped and looked back at me and sighed. "I think we need to find a place to lay low and you can learn a few things about your two halves and the magic that you will need to make it in this world, Ruby Red."

Turning once more, she headed off into the woods and away from the city. I glanced back wistfully at what was left of my old life and then followed her to wherever she was headed. I mean it wasn't like I had any other place to go, right?

# THE OLD MAN

It was almost dark when Joseph and his crew reached the house where the fae and her daughter had lived. Getting out of the SUV with the rest of his crew he was glad to see that only wolves were present in the area. Most humans may be stupid about Supernaturals, but they weren't total fools and with the body count starting to add up in this small town sooner or later the wrong person was bound to ask questions.

Joseph walked up to two Bellingham police officers that stood talking to one of his other crew leaders. The conversation between the three stopped as he stood in front of them. "Well, what happened here?"

Neither of the officers looked at Joseph and he could smell the fear emanating off of the two wolves who suddenly found the ground more interesting than the man who had just walked up on them. Joseph waited a few seconds then growled at the two men, resulting in both of them tearing their eyes from the ground and looking up at Joseph in even more fear if that was possible. "I asked what happened here, and someone had better answer now!"

One of the officers stepped forward but lost his courage and his eyes dropped to the ground. With no warning, Joseph grabbed the wolf by the throat and started to squeeze as he turned to the younger of the two officers and growled once more, "If you want to live, you will tell me what happened." And with that, a small sharp crack could be heard in the night coming from the shifter's throat held in Joseph's hand.

The young man watched as his partner's face started to turn blue under the administration of the leader's hand around his throat and he stammered, "Sir, we were parked down the road. When this crew didn't return after half an hour, we came up here and found them like this."

Joseph nodded and then released his hold on the shifter's throat he was holding and heard the thud of the body hitting the ground. Glaring at the younger officer, he patted him on the face as he whispered in the gathering night, "Now was that so hard?"

"No sir?"

"Good man. Now when your partner feels better, you get him up and get back down the road. Do you understand? I want no humans crashing our party."

"Yes sir," the younger officer stammered as a cold shiver raced up his spine. He watched his partner start to breathe once more as the injuries that he had sustained began to heal. Joseph and the first man that had been questioning the two officers moved off into the night.

The two of them moved with the grace of the hunter, moving through the woods with little noise left in their wake. The man next to Joseph kept quiet as they came to the first bundle in the leaves that could now be made out as a man's body minus the head. They stood there in an annoyed silence for a few minutes until the sound of an owl echoed in the dark. "You know, Joseph, he isn't going to like losing another crew."

Joseph glanced out of the side of his eyes at the man and a smile crept across his face. "Looking to take over my job, Harris?"

Harris shook his head in the negative and took a step back. "Oh hell no, you're the boss here."

Joseph looked the man full on and snarled, "Then don't worry about what he thinks, worry about what I think and get out there and catch this fae and the girl. That is after you get rid of these four pieces of trash." Then he turned and started back to his own SUV.

"Yes sir," Harris mumbled at Joseph's back and then turned to watch the other three shifters in his crew as they started to dig a hole in the ground big enough to fit four bodies and their separated heads.

OOOOO

Mack drove his small old Honda north up I-5 toward Bellingham with the windows down and the road trip music blasting into the cool night air. Mack had spent all day hitting up his contacts, Supernatural and human alike, with no hint of any fae that was in the organization's territory. There were, however, quiet whispers of something else, something more dangerous to the shifters than fae. So now he was headed up to the town where all the trouble seemed to be stemming from to check out just how accurate these whispers were.

As he thought about who he knew up in this part of the state, the thought flashed into his mind that he had a bad feeling that something was about to go down and that maybe this rat should just look out for himself and go a little further north after he hit Bellingham and cross the border into Canada.

But as soon as that idea came into his head he knew that it would be suicide to just take off, for the leader of this organization had the reputation of never letting anyone leave on their own accord. Look how Marcus had hunted that fae and her daughter for over eighteen years, he thought. No, when the shifter's leader wanted something or someone, he worried at it like a dog with a prized bone. Mack gave a little bark of laughter at that comparison.

No, he would just stick to the job and hunt down what the boss wanted and then hope for the best. With that sobering thought, he pushed up the speed of the old car as he headed north going over his contact list once more in his head, though from what he could see there wasn't any hint of a fae takeover of this territory.

OOOOO

We had been walking for hours up hills and through the woods, always avoiding anyone that would see us and report us to the police or anything else for that matter. Shane had been quiet the whole time since we left the area behind my house and I was just as happy to trudge along in silence.

I kept beating myself up in my mind over all the times that my mother and I had crossed words or I had made a nasty remark to her face or even behind her back. Now all I could think about was that I wished I had her back here right now and how I would do whatever she wanted me to. I guess you don't know just how much you are going to miss someone until they are gone.

I was lost in these dark thoughts not really paying attention to where we were going in the gathering darkness when I bumped into Shane's back eliciting a small huff from her. "Sorry," I whispered at the scowl she threw my way.

I glanced over her head at the edge of the clearing that we had come to and in the receding light I could just make out a small cabin across from us. It looked like it was growing out of the side a large hill that sat at the other edge of the clearing. I could see a small garden and an outhouse sitting not too far from the cabin.

The one dim light that shone from one window looked inviting, especially after the rough night and day I had had, but Shane seemed in no hurry to move any further toward it. "Who lives here?" I whispered, my curiosity getting the better of me.

Shane stiffened and started to turn her head toward me when a voice sounded out of the blackness of the woods behind us. "I live here and if you ladies are going to stand here all night I'm going in and have my dinner."

With that, a darker shadow walked past us and headed toward the cabin. Shane stood there for a second and then nodded her head toward where the old man was shuffling and followed him into the light shining from that window. I had no intention of staying out here by myself since I was getting eaten alive by mosquitoes anyways; so I followed the two of them toward the cabin.

Nearing the cabin, I passed a small hand pump that had a bucket under it catching the slow plinking drops of water dripping into it. I caught the sound of the water as a drop hit what was in the bucket, but was distracted by the stench coming from the outhouse as I passed it. Oh, I was so going to wait to go somewhere else before I walked out there into that little building to do my business. I heard a small chuckle from the old man and then his voice from the open door that lit up the cabin's yard said, "No fancy plumbing way out here, young lady."

Following the two through the door, I glanced around at

the minuscule cabin that could barely contain the three of us. To my left was a ladder that led up to a bunk that was just above the only table in the one room. To the right was a counter with a sink and some cabinets attached to the wall. On the back wall sat an old pot belly stove with a long thick black pipe running up through the ceiling of this tiny home. Hell, I think my bedroom back home was bigger than this place, of course, that brought to the forefront that I didn't have a bedroom anymore, or a home, or a mother for that fact.

"Make yourselves at home, ladies," the rough gravelly voice sounded from behind me. I turned just as the old man shut the door and leaned a crooked walking stick in the corner. I watched as he took off a light jacket and hung it on a hook above his stick and turned to face us with a small look of amusement.

Shane just shrugged her shoulders at me and slid under the bunk and onto a bench that surrounded three sides of the table. I glanced at the old man then at the fae and followed her example as she didn't seem too worried about him. "So you ladies hungry?" he asked as we got settled on the bench.

"Well yeah, but who . . ." I started to ask but stopped as the old man held up a hand and silenced me with a look.

"I never talk on an empty stomach. So we eat first, and then talk later."

I looked over at Shane who was sitting there ignoring the

conversation we were having, paying more attention to the small space we were in than in what we were saying. I couldn't for the life of me figure out what held her interest since we could see everything from where we sat, but I figured it was only polite to follow the old man's wishes since we were in his house. "Sure I guess – eat first, no problem, conversation later."

The old man turned and moved to the cabinets as he threw over his shoulder, "Good, cause I get grouchy when I'm hungry." Then I watched as he reached under the cabinet opposite of us and opened a door that hid a small fridge and pulled out three large slabs of meat from it.

Walking over to the stove, I saw him throw the meat into the biggest cast iron skillet that I had ever seen. It took up every inch of the stove, but still just barely held the thick slabs that had been deposited within it. Throwing a few pieces of wood into the stove, the flames inside grew and I could hear the sounds of meat starting to sizzle and the aroma of it cooking reminded me that it had been awhile since I had eaten.

All too soon the old man scooped up two of the steaks and slapped them down on the plates. Moving to the table where he slid one of the plates in front of me while glancing at Shane. "I know that you fae like your meat a little more well done so you can go and watch your dinner and get it when it suits your taste," he said as his nose wrinkled in distaste.

"Thanks," was all Shane muttered as she slid from her seat on the bench and walked over to the stove, going out of her way to ignore the two plates that the old man had set on the table. I looked down at my food swimming in a pool of red and for one second I felt my stomach do a flip. Then the smell of the undercooked meat hit my nose and I heard a grumble from down below. Suddenly I couldn't wait to sink my teeth into the meat before me, for some unknown reason.

Without thinking, a low growl escaped my lips as I grabbed the piece of meat in front of me and tore into with an overwhelming ferociousness. As I bit into the rare meat, I could feel the blood run down my throat and I savored that feeling. I couldn't help it, the feeling of tearing into prey and that smell of the wild just seemed to take over my senses. The hairs on my arms rose and my claws extended once more. I was so overcome by this wild animal feeling that I soon felt my canines elongate and this only served to help me rip the meat to bloody tatters with savage abandon.

I was soon done with the meal in front of me and looked up at the others in the room. Shane just stood at the stove watching me with certain wariness in her eyes, while the old man sat on his side of the bench with a sly smile crossing his face. Damn now where did that come from I wondered as I glanced down at my plate and the table in front of me covered in spots of red and slivers of meat. A large surprising belch erupted deep from within me. I whispered,

"Sorry," as I wiped my shirt sleeve across my mouth.

It was quiet in the room for a few seconds until the old man gave a small chuckle. "It's alright, young lady, it is all just part of the process."

"Is it always like this?" the fae whispered.

I glanced at the old man then at Shane who, by this time, had parked her butt on the counter and was eating her share of the meal straight out of the pan. I was a little hurt that she still had that look of wariness in her eyes and chose to sit across the room from me. Not that the room was all that big, but still it seemed like my new friend was leery of me all of a sudden. I looked back at the man and asked, "Okay I'll bite what is the process you're talking about and is what always like this?" I said glancing over at the fae and getting a little pissed that once more I felt like I was being left out of some big dark secret.

The old man glanced at the fae with a small look of annoyance. "No, it's not like this all the time." Then he gazed back at me with a puzzled look. "Your mother didn't talk to you about the change then?"

"NO, SHE DIDN'T TALK TO ME ABOUT ANY OF THIS AND I'M GETTING TIRED OF EVERYONE SEEMING TO KNOW WHAT IS GOING ON IN MY LIFE EXCEPT ME!" I yelled, my anger getting the best of me as I stood up from the table bumping my head on the bunk above me which only infuriated me even more.

The room got quiet after my outburst as both people stared at me again, one with that look of wariness, the other with a look of pity in those old eyes. I glared down at the table so that I could forgo seeing their eyes on me and slowly sat down again while I heard the old man clear his throat. "Sorry, young lady, I just assumed that you knew why your mother moved to this town since you were so close to your eighteenth birthday and the process is all."

I took a deep breath and looked up at the two, trying to keep my temper. I mean I don't know why I was so mad at these two since neither were the cause of all these changes in my life. In fact, all Shane had been doing all day long was help to keep me alive and this old man didn't seem like much of a threat. "Look, I'm sorry okay? I just feel . . ."

The old man cleared his throat and laid his hand on my arm. I felt the warmth and comfort that he was trying to pass on to me, but a tiny growl slipped out of my lips, as though I was giving an enemy a warning. The old man chuckled once more and pulled his hand back to his side of the table. "Sorry," I whispered wondering where that had come from.

"Don't worry about it, young lady, cats and dogs usually ruffle each other's fur wrong sometimes, especially when one is close to their first change over, and edgy, bad-tempered, and rude were probably the words you were looking for," he said as he sat back in his chair and I glared at him. "Now you want to know why your mother brought you to this town and what the process is?" he said with another chuckle at my look like he could really care less what I thought of him.

"Yes. That would be nice to know," I said with a scowl at the old man's smile.

"Aright then, you do know that you are half-shifter, right?"

"Duh, that's obvious from what Shane has told me and from the little, uhm, changes that I have been going through since last night."

The old man looked at me for a second, his smile leaving his face to be replaced by some small underlying look that said that he just might be more dangerous than he looked. I glanced down at the table, breaking eye contact as he went on with his explanation. "As I was saying, you are half-shifter. When a shifter reaches the age of eighteen on the first full moon they go through the process of change and that is why your mother brought you to this town."

I looked up, puzzled at why this small town was so special out of all the others that we had lived in. "Okay, I'll bite why here?"

The smile came back on to the old man's face as he pointed to himself. "This place is special because of me," he said with a quiet laugh and a note of pride. I looked at him seeing nothing but an old grizzled man sitting across from me and the skepticism must have been written all over my face as he continued to talk. "You see, young lady, your mother was fae and didn't know what to expect at the change. So she was going to bring you to me so that I could help you with the process and make sure that you didn't hurt yourself or anyone else for that matter, but she should have told you beforehand what was going on. It does make it easier when the person knows about the change and has some idea of what to expect."

I glanced over at Shane and then back at the old man. "Okay, and you know about what happens at this change because why?" I said then hopped out of my seat, hitting my head once more, but not really caring as I backed into the corner, a low growl issuing from deep within my chest as the old man before me started to shift. It happened so fast – one minute he sat there an old man and the next I was looking into the eyes of the biggest cat I had ever seen. Then he went back to being an old man again.

I tried to bring my breathing back to normal as I stared at the old man and pictured the creature that he had turned into. I saw the mangy, tawny hide of the cat and the long saber-like teeth that hung down from his lips and sputtered, "You're some sort of a cougar?"

"I prefer mountain lion if you don't mind, 'cougar' has such a negative connotation in the human world especially as it describes some older human females."

I heard a snort of laughter from across the room and the old man threw Shane a dirty look. "Careful fae, you are not needed here anymore and would make a small tasty snack."

Shane reached behind her and started to pull out one of her

swords as I watched the old man start to change back to his cat form when I jumped between the two of them. "Okay enough you two, I need to find out more about this change stuff and the two of you fighting isn't helping me get answers."

I watched as Shane reluctantly put up her sword and the old man reversed his change back to his human form. "You're right, young lady; we don't have time for this. I'm sorry, fae, for my manners for sometimes I can be an old grouch living alone as I do," he said this as he gave a slight bow toward the fae.

Shane just gave a little bow back and whispered, "And I am sorry for my bad manners in your home, sir."

It was nice that these two looked like they were not going to rip each other's throats out now. But the later the night wore on, the more I had this uneasy sensation like an itching, crawling feeling that had started all up and down my body. The old man looked at me and then at Shane and announced, "I think she is close. You need to come with me, young lady, and trust me."

I didn't know where he wanted to go, but if it would get rid of this sensation I was all for it. "Okay, where are we going and what are we doing when we get there?"

The old man smiled and closed the drapes on the one window of the cabin and walked over to the still hot smoldering stove. He reached in back of it and pushed down on the molding of the wall and a door opened behind the stove. He turned back to the two of us and smiled as he said, "You two young ladies just follow me and I will show you where we are going." And with that, he disappeared behind the stove and into the dark.

# THE CHANGE

Mack knocked on the door and waited in the dark. A dim light lit up the porch as a face looked out from the old house at his visitor. The man took a few seconds to recognize who was standing on his doorstep in the middle of the night and his shoulders fell at the sight of the shifter. The face behind the door's window disappeared, the light went out, and Mack waited as the sound of locks clicked on the other side of the door.

"What are you doing here?" a low voice whispered from the partially opened door.

"Nice to see you too, John. Let me in, we have some talking to do."

John stood there looking at Mack for a few seconds then closed the door and the rat shifter could hear the sound of chains moving against the wood. The door opened just enough for the unwanted visitor to slip into the hallway. Before closing it, the owner of the house glanced around his front yard and then slammed the door behind them. Turning to the man in front of him he held his voice to a whisper. "What do you want, Mack?"

"Well first off are we going to stand here in the hallway and talk or are you going to invite me into your home?"

John stood there and then looked down the hallway where the sound of kid's laughter could be heard. "You're in my house or as far as you're going to be, so ask your questions here in the hallway and then go. I don't need trouble from you or your friends."

Mack sighed and then listened to the sounds coming from further in the house, understood John's apprehension and nodded. "Alright have it your way but this is no way to treat a friend. Have you heard anything about fae up here in Bellingham?"

A quick bark of laughter issued from John. "Seriously 'friend', you drove up all the way from Seattle just for rumors of fae? The fae here in Bellingham, are you nuts?"

"Fine nothing about fae then how about vamps?" Mack knew he had scored a point as the man in front of him looked down at the floor in fright. "John, tell me or I'll have to have someone else come and talk to you, and you know that they won't be as nice as I am to you or your family."

With a quick glance at the shifter and then toward the living room, John growled, "Don't threaten me, rat." But then John's shoulders caved in. "Alright, Mack just don't send the wolves from Seattle up here. The ones that we have living up here are bad enough, okay?"

Mack nodded and then glanced at his watch. "Now tell me what you have heard."

"It's going around town that some shifters were killed last night, and that they may have been killed by some vamp from down California way."

Mack looked at the man standing in front of him in the hallway and then shook his head. "It was a fae that did in the shifters last night. Where did you hear about this vamp?"

"All I know Mack is that there is a vamp in town and looking for some girl."

Mack was startled by that piece of news. "Dam . . ." but his voice froze as a small child came running into the hall, its laughter floating and following it from the other room.

The child stopped and looked at her father and the man standing next to him, her innocent eyes going wide at the sight of Mack. "Daddy? Mommy said it was time for bed."

John looked at his daughter then glanced at Mack as a low growl of warning issued from his throat. His daughter slowly backed up a few steps and then turned and ran back toward where she had come from. The rat shifter took a step back from John for even a lowly shifter like the one before him could be dangerous if they thought their kittens were in danger. "I'll go now John, but keep an ear out for anything else going on in this town. Got me?"

The bravado left John's eyes as he reached over and opened the door for the other man and as the rat shifter slipped out the door he mumbled something about wolves and their pets. Mack just ignored the other man and stood on the steps of the house as he heard the locks on the door being replaced. First fae and now a vamp, yeah maybe it is time to leave this territory for good, he thought, as he headed out into the night to meet some more of his contacts.

OOOOO

Shane and I followed the old man into the dark recess behind the stove. Once we were through, I could feel the man shut the door and we all stood in the pitch dark until I heard the flick of a switch and we were bathed in a dim light coming from above us.

We stood in a narrow cave opening that led about five feet over to another door. I looked around and saw that I was right, the cabin we had been in was built right up to the side of the rock face which hid the cave behind it. "Nice room. Did you decorate it yourself?" I said as I looked around and then down at the door at the other side of the cave.

The old man laughed. "Feisty little puppy, aren't you? Well, your kind usually is before they go through the change. Now follow me, young ladies." And with that, he walked to the door, reaching into his pocket and pulling out a jumble of keys.

So since he asked so nicely and we didn't have anywhere else to go, we followed the old man to the door. I watched him unlock it and move the door aside. From the weight of it and the old man's struggles, I figured it was pretty sturdy and was proved right as we walked in the room behind it. The door was made of heavy wood and banded together with iron and silver studs. The old man confirmed that fact when he turned to Shane and chuckled as he warned her not to cut herself on the door and I saw how he was very careful not to touch any of the silver himself.

The fae never said a word, but just raised an eyebrow up and gave that old man one of those looks that said, 'Don't worry about me, old man, I can take care of myself.'

I sighed, shook my head at those two and walked past them and into the dark room beyond the door. I once more heard the flick of a switch and this time the light lit up the room so that I could get a good look at it. To one side there was a small opening leading to a cage while on the other side was a living area with bunks and a tiny kitchen.

I did a quick look around while that itchy, crawling feeling started getting worse as the night wore on. "Okay, now what?" I said turning to Shane and the old man.

The old man looked at me, smiled, and walked over to the cage door while putting on a pair of gloves. He opened it and with a bow and a sweep of his hand pointed inside and said, "Why now, young lady, you go in here for tonight until your first change is over."

I started to back up as I saw Shane shift over toward the door leading out. "Oh hell no. No way am I going in there, and I'm not going to be some zoo animal you two can stare at all night. No way, no how."

Shane, blocking the only way to escape, tensed as though ready to spring into action if I made a break for it while the old man stood at the cage door, the smile now gone from his face. "I'm sorry young lady, but you need to get inside now. Tonight. This is the first night of the full moon and we have no idea what you are capable of since you are of mixed blood."

I looked at the two and once more at the cage door that the old man still held open. That feeling I've had all night long now really increasing almost like I could feel hairs under my skin trying to break out, but I tried to give it one more try. "What? You guys act like I'm something that has never happened before. Surely there has been someone before like me a half and half, hasn't there?"

The old man shook his head and then swept his arm toward the cage once more without saying anything else to me. I glanced back at the fae and saw that I definitely wasn't going through that door, shrugged my shoulders and headed to the cage. I stopped before going through the door and looked at the two of them. "You know, if nothing happens tonight you two owe me a big apology."

Shane stood there in stony silence and just nodded her head toward the cage. I glanced at the old man and then at the cage and then back at the fae who still guarded the only way out of the room. Suddenly this weird vibe came over me, screaming that the fae in front of me was prey. I could see the pulsing of her heart beating in her neck and I took one step toward her, my mouth watering at the thought of sinking my teeth into her.

I heard a low cough of warning from the old man that bought me back to reality. I shook my head to clear it of these thoughts and stepped into the cage as he slammed and locked the door behind me. Yeah, I really needed to be somewhere safe as I turned once more and my eyes caught the heartbeat in the fae's neck from across the room.

"Okay now wharrooo. . ." I slammed my mouth shut as my question turned into a wolf's howl. Oh damn, I am in deep trouble now as the two came closer to the cage door. I now know what the poor animals at the zoo feel like as I watched the old man and Shane stare at me intently. Well maybe more like a science experiment than a zoo animal – I grimaced at that thought.

I felt an overpowering urge to lunge and grab one of them and take a bite out of their tasty bodies, in fact as that thought crossed my mind my mouth started to water again and I felt my claws and canines once more extend. I started to lunge across the cage when I felt like I hit a brick wall my body slamming to the ground in intense pain.

OOOOO

The fae and the old man watched as Ruby Red started to jump across the cage at them. Her body stopped in mid-air and then hit the floor. Legs drawn up into her chest with her arms wrapped around her body, the sound of popping ligaments and muscles echoing off the walls. They could hear her groan in pain and then scream as flesh, torn clothes, and fur flew into the air. Both of them took a step back so that they were not hit by the gunk that flew through the air. "Old man, is it supposed to happen like that?"

The old man glanced at the fae standing next to him, her two swords now in her hands. Her eyes were wide as they watched the figure, that was once a young girl, stand up and stare out at them with yellow eyes. "No, it definitely is not supposed to happen quite like that, young lady."

A low growl issued from the creature before them and each involuntarily took a step back. Shane took in the creature and tried to picture what seconds ago was the young redhead that had entered the cage. It was a little unnerving to see something that was a cross between a wolf and a human standing there in front of her. She glanced at the old man and was glad that she wasn't the only one that was having problems with the sight before her. "I thought that when you shifters change you take on a purely animal shape? I mean she is . . ."

The old man chuckled and looked at the fae and then back

at the, for want of a better word, monster before him. "Yeah I used to watch those old monster movies that humans made and she looks like she could have stepped right out from one of them, doesn't she?"

Shane thought back to some of those movies the old man was talking about and gave her own chuckle at how right he was. Ruby Red did look like someone's nightmares come to life. She was now six feet tall looking like she was all claws, bulging muscles, and teeth; her long canines reflecting the light of the room. As experienced a fighter as the fae was, she was glad that the creature was on that side of the cage. "Okay, old man, so now what do we do?" Then she looked closer at the claws and saw that they seemed to alternate between shiny silver and the dullness of cold iron. Interesting that Ruby Red's body seemed to adjust her defenses according to those creatures around her, she thought.

The old man glanced at the creature standing in the cage looking at them like they were nothing more than its next meal then over at Shane as he took a step toward the cage. "Well I guess we should see just how much of her is in there now, don't you think?"

Shane's eyes got bigger as she took in the creature, then she took a deep breath and stepped toward the cage with the old man. "Yeah, just be careful because those claws of hers could make either of us very dead or at the very least shred us to bits and make us wish we were dead." The old man looked closer at the creature's claws and agreed with the fae, but stepped to the bars of the cage anyway.

OOOOO

The pain, the itching, the skin crawling feeling got so bad as I lay on the ground and then a sudden explosion of relief came over me and I could feel the power flow throughout my body. As I gradually climbed to my feet, I could sense the changes in my body; feel the muscles and the power of them giving me the confidence that I could take on the world and tear it apart bit by bit.

I looked out of the cage through new eyes, seeing now looks not of fear, but of wariness from the two that stood before me. Then I smiled as I could smell just a suggestion of the underlying fear there. Then a hint of the wild woods tainted my nostrils. Somewhere in this cave, there was another opening or maybe just a crack in the rocks that was letting in a minute breeze, just enough to carry that smell.

I observed the two as they watched me, waiting to see what they would do. I listened to them talk about the creature, the creature that was me. Glancing down at my body, I could see the dark red fur that covered it keeping me warm and covered since what I had been wearing was now spread all over the cage's floor. I flexed my new muscles, loving that feeling of raw power and wildness that now flowed through my veins.

The two people, no not people, creatures of the night just as I was, but different. The older one, I could smell the odor of cat on him, the smell of the wild outdoors was there also. The other, smaller one with the swords wasn't a shifter; she had a different kind of scent, a smell of magic with a little bit of darkness mixed in.

I gave a low warning growl and both stopped where they stood with the little one giving off the faintest scent of fear again. Fear of me, fear of what I had become. God, I could almost taste that fear it was so real and so good. Then the old man spoke. "How are you feeling, young lady?"

I glanced at the two for a few seconds, a look of worry crossing both of their faces until I answered back. "I'm fine," I said, my body not the only thing that had changed as my voice echoed in the cave, a low roll of thunder mixed in with a growl.

The look of relief on both their faces was almost comical to watch as they stood there, each lost in their own thoughts. A tiny feeling of the two before me as my prey, of the need to rip them apart, surged up within me. I fought it down and remembered that they were here to help me through this experience. It wouldn't be a great start to this shifter thing if I started to eat my friends. Well . . . no, NO! Definitely, can't eat them. "Now what do we do?" I asked.

The old man moved closer to the bars of the cage and gave me a piercing look. "Now, my, um, young lady, we let this first change process complete itself, and then we see how you feel in the morning."

I nodded my head and looked around the cage. There wasn't much to it, just a part of the larger cave that had the bars thrown across it. I could see that the ends of the metal bars had been buried deep within the rock wall. I fought the urge once more to test their strength and break through to eat those in front of me. I guess this was going to be a little harder than I figured it would be. I could only hope that these feelings would dampen down with time. I really hated the thought of having to be locked up every time there was a full moon out. Then I caught another whiff of something, something in the bars. Silver, I could smell that the bars were made of silver. So that's why the old man had put on gloves to open the door. I smiled, somehow knowing, even in this form, that they would never hurt me. Yes, if I really wanted to, I knew deep down I could get at both of them and tear them apart before either could react. For some reason, this more than anything else seemed to settle my wild nature down a bit.

The old man looked at me and then glanced back at the fae who had moved over to one of the bunks on the other side of the room. "I hope you don't mind, but usually I don't get to ask questions of the shifters that come to me for help since we all shift into animal form."

"Yeah, I guess it does make it a little hard to communicate."

The old man laughed quietly. "Yeah it does, but usually with a wolf shifter after the first change they have this sort of pack communication. You know how, when they are changed, they can communicate with those in their own pack."

"That makes it handy, I guess, but what about you? I mean can you communicate or talk to other cats?"

The old man shrugged his shoulders. "We are solitary creatures, us cats. When we cross each other's path we can use a form of communication, but it is fuzzy and not very reliable so we usually stay out of each other's way. That seems to keep misunderstandings down to a minimum . . . also deaths."

"So I guess I'm the only one with verbal skills after I shift is what you are telling me?"

"Yeah, I've never seen anything like you before, and believe me I have been around a long time, young lady."

"Alright then I have a quick question for you," I said concentrating on our conversation which seemed to be keeping down those wild urges that kept creeping up from deep within me, stronger and stronger. "Will I only change on the full moon? I mean when Jason attacked me and changed it wasn't a full moon out that night."

The old man stood there for a few seconds before answering my question. "No, usually the first change doesn't happen until the first full moon after the shifter's eighteenth birthday, but afterward they are able to change anytime that they want – depending on how strong of a shifter they are. Though with you, we may have to wait and see."

"Because I'm half fae, right?"

"Yes, young lady, because you are half fae, and because we can't be sure how strong you really are until the next time you want to change," he said with another of his small laughs.

"What's so funny, old man?"

The old man looked at me and then glanced behind him at the bunk where Shane now was laying, a soft snore coming from her direction. "Well, young lady, it's just that I don't think we really have to worry too much about how strong of a shifter you are with how fast you seemed to have gone through the change."

"Oh," was all I could get out thinking back to when Jason had changed it had seemed like it took a little longer than when I had. Of course, he had been hurt at the time so maybe that counted for the time difference. "So you're saying the faster you can change the stronger the shifter?"

"Yeah that and you seemed in a whole lot less pain than what most shifters go through when they change the first time around."

I don't know where he got that idea from because I remembered being in a whole hell of a lot of pain when I changed, but I guess this was another one of those things that I needed to take his word for.

The old man must have seen the look of doubt on my face for he laughed again causing a small ripple of anger to surface and a little growl slipped out. "Now don't get your fur all in a fluff, young lady. Believe me, when a shifter changes, especially on the first one, they are not ready to stand up and rip the world apart like you looked to do."

I was a little mollified by the old man's answer, but still, the creature side of me didn't like to be laughed at and it was hard to fight the urge to lunge at the cage and take apart my new friend. "Alright, it's just that it's strange to have all these feelings going on inside of me right now." I looked around the cage and then back at the old man. "And being caged up like an animal in the zoo isn't helping them either."

The old man walked over to a shelf and took down a dusty old bottle and started to pour it into a glass as he said, "Yeah I know, but believe me it is for your own good. This way you don't start out your life as a shifter that killed someone close to you."

Not much I could say after that as I didn't really want to know what he was talking about. Even though, from the look on his face, I figured that I had a pretty good idea that he was talking about himself. Yeah, I know it might have been a little selfish of me, but right now I had this whole changing into the big bad monster thing to deal with.

The old man really didn't seem to want to talk about it more anyway as he pushed the glass through the bars of the cage and then took a couple of steps back. "Here drink this down and it will make you feel better."

I glanced at the glass of liquid and then back up at the old man. "What is it?"

The old man smiled without a laugh this time and said, "Just a little something to help with the change, now just chug it down, young lady."

I reached over and picked up the glass and swirled it around – which was a big mistake – as a putrid smell issued from the glass. I set the glass down and shook my head at the old man. "Oh hell no. That smells like sewer water and not good sewer water either."

The old man stood there for a second and then started to reach into the cage for the glass. "Well okay then, but don't come crying to me when you change back. Man, I remember the first time I changed back, never felt that much pain in my . . ."

I grabbed the glass and slammed it back with the stench of the concoction floating around my face. I barely managed to swallow the stuff down without it coming back up. As I put the glass down, the cage narrowed into a black tunnel and as I felt my head hit the floor I heard the old man's laughter. "Works every time." As the darkness overcame me, I promised that that old man would pay for that little trick of his.

# VAMP

Joseph watched the morning sun rise over the mountains and wished for nothing else than to find a place to sleep. As he stretched, he could hear his bones creak and the muscles pop from the recent change that he had gone through. After leaving the scene of his crew's massacre, he and the other shifters with him had changed to their wolf forms to be able to track their prey better, or so he thought.

Unfortunately for the two crews of enforcers, the fae with Marcus's daughter had used some kind of magic to erase their tracks and they were lost somewhere within the town or the surrounding mountains and forest. As much as Joseph loved the wild he wished he was back in Seattle where he could flood the town with shifters. That way, no matter what kind of magic the fae used, their chances of finding the two of them were better than in this little town. There was just too much wild country up this way. The two he sought could hide forever from the small crews he had with him.

Now as the dawn sun continued rising over the mountains and bathing the clearing they were in with its morning glow, Joseph watched the three members of his crew stretch and move around their vehicle as they waited for the others to show up. The three shifters tensed then relaxed as Joseph raised his hand a little as the slight breeze brought the smell of another creature to their noses.

A few minutes later, Joseph cocked his head at a noise from the bushes at the side of the road and smiled. "You can come out now, rat, we know that you are here. We smelled your stench when you left your car down the road."

Mack stepped out of the bushes and then glanced over at the other three shifters that were casually moving toward him and cutting off any escape. "I just wanted to make sure that you were the people that I needed to talk to is all, Joseph."

Joseph looked at the rat shifter and slid closer to him in the blink of an eye, causing Mack to step back and bump into the other wolf that was now standing right behind him. "Marcus doesn't trust you, rat, and that makes me not trust you. Why are you here?"

Mack looked down at the ground, trying not to make eye contact with those that were now surrounding him. It was never a good idea to challenge a just changed werewolf when they were still cranky from the stress of the process.

Of course with these enforcers, it was never a good idea to challenge them anytime since they all seemed to have hair trigger tempers that could explode at any second for no reason at all. "I'm here at Marcus's request to find out about any fae in the area, I . . ."

"I know that, rat," Joseph snarled as he took out some of his frustrations out on the smaller and weaker shifter. His temper frazzled by the lack of success at finding his prey and now the lateness of his last crew wasn't doing much for his mood. "I mean what are you doing here on this spot right now?" the wolf's growl ratcheting up a notch higher.

Mack quickly glanced up and then back down at the ground knowing that the news he was bearing would not be good and these wolves tended to kill creatures that brought news that they didn't want to hear. With a deep gulp of air the rat shifter whined, "Now it wasn't me, but I found them and I just thought that you should know . . ."

Joseph's hand flicked out and wrapped around Mack's throat as he raised him until the rat's feet were dangling just inches off the ground. "You mean to tell me, rat, that you found the fae and the leader's daughter and you didn't tell me first thing?"

With another flick of his wrist, the rat flew by the other wolves and hit the side of the black SUV, denting the door with his body and then sliding slowly down to the ground. As Mack's bottom touched the gravel, he blacked out for a few seconds as the pain of being choked and then thrown into the unmoving solid object racked his whole body. Coming to a few seconds later, he glanced up at the four wolves that now surrounded him and then looked down at the ground he was sitting on before croaking out, "No, I didn't find the fae and the girl. But I know where your other crew is. I found them or what is left of them, that is."

Joseph knelt down, causing Mack to flinch which brought laughter from the other three wolves standing around. With a quick, venomous look from Joseph, the laughter was cut short as their leader once more turned to the rat shifter. "Sorry about that, rat; now, tell me where my crew is, if you don't mind," he whispered in a quiet dangerous voice that Mack knew the wolves only used when they were trying to keep tight control on the anger that was boiling just below the surface.

Mack hesitated for a second, which brought another snarl from Joseph before he pointed down the road he had just come up. "Your crew is about two miles down this road and about two hundred feet into the woods on the right side of the road."

Joseph reached over and grabbed Mack's shirt and lifted him off the ground as though the rat shifter had no weight at all and set him on his feet. "Alright, rat, what did you mean before when you said 'what is left of them'?"

Mack didn't want to be the bearer of this bad news, but as the hand tightened on his shirt he gave a small squeal of fright and spilled all he knew to the wolf before him. "All four are dead. It looks like a vamp got to them."

"You had better hope it was a vamp, rat, and that you're not playing games or you will be sorry." With that, Joseph threw the rat shifter once more against the black SUV and motioned for two of his crew to go check out Mack's story.

Mack slowly slid down the truck door once more and sat on the ground wishing for the tenth time in the last couple of days that he had just kept going to the border and straight into Canada. Not that the grizzly shifters up there were any easier to deal with, but there were far fewer of them and they were inclined to leave the other shifters to own devices except, of course, when they tended to eat one.

The third shifter of the crew stood over Mack and watched as the other two wolves took off at a slow jog down the road that the rat had traversed only a little while ago. Joseph though ignored the rat and stood in the middle of the clearing where the two vehicles were parked with his arms crossed behind his back and his eyes drawn to the ground before him.

About half an hour later, all eyes were looking up the road once more as the two shifters returned. By the way they were walking and the worried looks that they kept throwing over their shoulders, Joseph and the other wolf became more alert and started to shift their own eyes around to the trees that surrounded them.

Both shifters made a beeline toward Joseph and stood

before him, still throwing glances over their shoulders until their leader snarled, "Well was the rat right?"

The bigger of the two shifters just nodded as his companion gave his report. "Yeah, he was right, Joseph. There are vamp signs all over the place and the whole crew was drained."

Joseph turned and looked at the rat sitting on the ground. "Damn! Well did he have anything to do with it?" he asked as he pointed in Mack's direction.

This time both shifters shook their head at their leader's question while the smaller of the two answered, "No, his scent comes in from the road and leaves straight out to the road again, hours after they were killed."

Joseph stood there thinking for a few minutes about what it all meant in the grand scheme of things and how it could change his actions. None of the wolves made a sound or move for they don't want to interrupt until Joseph has a plan worked out while Mack was hoping to escape the notice of the shifter for a while longer.

Finally, the shifter looks up from the ground and points at the two in front of him. "You two take their vehicle and get rid of their bodies, but. . ." he said as the two shifters start to move out then stop. "I want you to be very careful. At the first sign of trouble you go to the hotel and wait for us to get there, you got me?"

Both shifters nod and move toward the second SUV while

Joseph walked over to Mack still sitting on the ground, trying for all he was worth to stay out of the leader's notice. "Get up, rat," the leader snarled.

Mack slowly gathered himself from the ground and stood, his eyes still diverted downward. Joseph stepped closer to the rat shifter and reached out with his hand and raised the shifter's head so that they were now looking eye to eye. "Rat, if I find out that you had anything to do with this you will wish I gave you a quick death when I'm through with you. Do you understand me?"

Mack nodded feeling the grip of the wolf shifter tighten on his chin for a second then the pressure let up as Joseph pushed past him and climbed into the black SUV with his companion. Mack hastily moved aside, just barely missing getting ran over by the wolves as the vehicle spun out of the clearing and headed back to town throwing mud and rocks all over the rat. "Damn wolves," the rat swore as he headed back down the road toward his own vehicle.

OOOOO

I slowly blinked my eyes open as muted morning sunlight shown through the frilly white curtains of my bedroom. I sat up suddenly, the pink comforter sliding off my body and piling around my waist as I looked around the room. This was not my room, it looked like someone had dumped Pepto all over the walls. From downstairs, I could hear my mother singing and the banging of pots and pans in the kitchen.

Slowly I walked out of my room and down the steps and stopped at the kitchen door looking at a sight I'd never seen before. My mother stood before the stove, a smile lighting her face, wearing a frilly white apron. "Hello Ruby, it's about time you got up young lady," my mother said cheerfully.

I rubbed my eyes and then blinked them a couple times but the picture of domestic tranquility never changed. This whole scene could have come out of some cheesy 1950s TV show. "What are you doing, Mother?"

"Why I'm making you breakfast, of course," my mother chirped in a voice I'd never heard before.

I slowly walked into the kitchen and sat at the table as my mother pranced over and set a full plate of food down in front of me. As she twirled away from me and sat down across the table, I closed my eyes and slowly shook my head to rid myself of this impossible vision. "Is something wrong, dear?" that bubbly voice sounded in my ears again.

I opened my eyes and tried to make sense of what I was seeing. "Is this a dream, I mean you're . . ." I stopped at the words I dreaded to say, hoping with all my heart that somehow the other parts of the day had been the dream or should I say a nightmare?

"Not exactly a dream, more like a favor. The One granted me one last chance to see you and to explain, my dear," my mother said as the frilly apron disappeared and the cheerful look left her face. "You saw me as you wanted me to be, but this is the real me."

"I'm sorry for that, mother. I think I understand now. I know you made the best choices you could along the way."

"I'm sorry, Ruby, that I won't be there to help you along with the burden that will be your future. But you have to know that everything I did, I did out of love – the only love one of my kind could show."

"Wait, I need to know more about this burden I carry. What future? What are you talking about?"

My mother turned her head away but not before I saw two tears slowly slide down her pale cheeks. As I watched, my mother and the room around us started to fade.

OOOOO

I sluggishly opened my eyes to the light that was glaring down from the ceiling of the cage. I could feel every muscle and tendon in my body ache with a dull pounding as I sat up. The good thing was that my two friends hadn't left me lying naked on the cold floor but had covered me with a smelly old green army blanket. The bad thing was that as I sat up the blanket started to fall and as I grabbed it to keep a tiny bit of modesty; the sudden movement elicited a groan of pain that lanced throughout my whole body and brought a small chuckle from outside the cage door.

"I've had several mornings like that, young lady. Sometimes from the change and others . . . well, let's just say I probably should have drunk less than I did. Give it a few minutes and the pain will go down." I looked up toward the voice that spoke from the open door of the cage and could make out the fuzzy outline of the old man standing there looking down at me. I felt like my whole body had one giant migraine, the flu and a hangover all at once.

I tried to say something, but all that came out was this weird dry rasping sound. My throat was in as bad a condition as the rest of me and in no state to make the correct sounds. The old man stepped forward and held out a glass that I eyed with some suspicion, especially after last night's little trick. "It's only water, young lady, I promise. Part of the pain you feel is from being dehydrated. Drink this and you will start to feel better."

I moved my hand out to the cool glass, each diminutive movement hurting and sending that pain throughout every little molecule of my body. I took a sniff of the liquid and then a small sip and found out that the glass did indeed just have water in it. Ice cold pure water that trickled down my throat and was sucked up into my thirsty tissues before it could hit my stomach. I had never tasted anything as sweet as that water. Of course, it could have a little bit to do with the whole changing into a monster thing and all, but right then I didn't care as I held the cold glass to my forehead.

I wanted to just gulp down the liquid in the glass as my body screamed for more of the water, but I sipped it slowly as I eyed the old man who was standing there watching me with that same cautious look that he had worn last night.

"What?" I asked a few minutes later as I put the empty glass down on the floor of the cage.

The old man smiled and stepped back out of the cage and motioned toward a small door that stood open at the back of the cave. "There's a bathroom in there where you can wash up and also some clothes for you to throw on. When you're done, I'll make you some breakfast."

I sat there looking at him then glanced at the door. My stomach growled at the word 'breakfast' and told me that the water was nice, but some food would be better. Wrapping the blanket around me as I stood, I could feel the coarse material stick to me in places where it was very uncomfortable. The thought flashed through my brain that a nice hot shower would be good, followed by wondering if I was always going to feel this gross after each change. I stopped just before I got to the bathroom door and looked around the cave as something was missing. It took a few seconds for my thoughts to connect and then I figured it out. "Where's Shane?"

The old man stopped digging in the fridge and glanced my way while pulling a plate of four large steaks from its inside. "Don't worry, the fae will be back. She went out to make sure that your tracks were covered and that there were no wolves around. Now go get cleaned up."

I glanced around once more and then zeroed in on the raw meat that was lying on the plate and with a low growl took a step toward the old man and away from the bathroom. I could smell the raw, red blood from across the room and my mouth was watering. Then his loud voice caught my attention, "Clean up first, eat afterward, young lady, and you will feel better. Now move it or I'll eat it all myself."

I felt another involuntary growl escape my lips at that but turned and stalked into the bathroom, slamming the door behind me. I know it was childish, but I was never known for being even-tempered even before finding out that I was half-werewolf.

I showered quickly partly due to the fact that I was hungry but mostly due to the fact that the shower was as cold as the glass of water that I had drunk a couple of minutes ago. Using the rock of soap that was on a small shelf, I washed off all the gunk and bits of fur and other things I'd rather not think about that were stuck on various parts of my body.

The water may have been coming straight off of a glacier, but it did the trick and finally I was clean. After drying off on an old towel that looked like it had been cut off from the same coarse green blanket I had slept with I threw on the clothes that the old man had left for me. The smells wafting under the door from the cooking steaks urged me to hurry and I didn't even give a second's thought that once again the pile of clothes had been minus a few things like undergarments. Oh well, I thought, as I opened the door, at least what I did have on fit and I was clean. I hated to admit it but the old man was right, I did feel better after getting cleaned up from last night's little change.

Stepping out of the bathroom, I could see that Shane had returned and that she was sitting on the top bunk eating what looked like a plate of mushrooms and other assorted veggies. As I watched her crunch on a carrot, I looked over at where the old man was just shifting three of the steaks I had seen onto one plate. He walked over and set the plate on an undersized table with a single chair that was sort of stuck in a small corner of the cave without a word and then went back to the stove.

I wanted to rush over and bury my teeth into the pile of meat but tried to keep my dignity as I made myself slowly shuffle over and stand behind the chair. My stomach gave a low rumble of protest and I could hear a small snigger from both of my 'friends'. "Well don't just stand there, young lady, sit down and eat before your stomach jumps out of your body and does it for you."

I sat down and cut off a slim piece and placed the rare meat into my mouth. Oh hell, who am I kidding calling it 'rare', it was all but raw, but at this point, I didn't care and my stomach growled once more. I savored each bite that I shoved into my mouth. Soon my knife and fork were scraping a bare plate and I looked up at the old man who was sitting across from me, his own plate as empty as mine. "Feel better now, young lady, after getting all cleaned up and fed?"

"Yeah sure, I guess. Even though I still feel like I can eat more."

The old man nodded. "Yeah I know, shifters are always hungry – especially after they change. It's our higher running metabolism, but give it a little bit to sit on your stomach and I'll get you some more in a little while. Okay?"

I shrugged my shoulders since he was the expert and then glanced at Shane, who was still munching on her veggie tray on the bunk she had chosen for her eating spot. "So did you find any werewolves following our trail?"

The fae did a quick glance at the old man and then looked at me. "Yeah I found what was left of a werewolf crew."

"What was left of them? What happened to the wolves?"

"Vamp," was all Shane said then she looked down at her plate and started to munch once again on the veggies. I stared at her and figured that I wasn't going to get anything else from her so I turned to the old man. "Okay, 'vamp' as in vampire, like bloodsucking undead that rise at night sort of 'vamp'?"

The old man laughed at my expression as Shane popped her head up from her plate and threw daggers with her eyes at the old man. "It's not funny, old man. We got enough trouble here with the shifters without adding a vamp to the mix."

The laughter stopped at Shane's rebuke. The old man sat there and watched the both of us for a few seconds. "Yeah you're right, fae. Forgive me for making fun of the both of you. I am usually alone so sometimes I let my warped sense of humor get the better of me, but you're right a vamp isn't something to make fun of."

I looked between the two of them and saw that they seemed to have made some measure of peace between them during the night, as each just nodded at the other. The fae once more went back to munching on her carrots while the old man seemed to drift off deep in his own thoughts.

Listening to the silence of the cave, silent except for the quiet crunching coming from the bunk, two thoughts crossed my mind. One was how could Shane seriously eat that rabbit food and the other was that I really needed to find out what in the hell was happening in the world, cause it sure wasn't the one that I had been living in just a couple of days ago.

I watched as the old man sighed and then focused his attention on me and shook his head. "I imagine that you want to know what is going on and what all this has to do with you, don't you."

I nodded not trusting my voice, hoping that, finally, I was going to get some answers to the questions that had been running through my head since the night I had found out that the things that go bump in the night are real and not just some story made up to scare kids.

# HISTORY LESSON

Mack sat in his car for a half hour, going over all the info that he had collected down in Seattle and up here in Bellingham. No matter how he looked at it when he got back to the organization he figured once he shared the news he had gathered for Marcus he would have a very violent but hopefully quick end. Of course, knowing the wolves as he did he was sure of the first option but not so sure of the second.

Finally after sitting and trying to figure out alternatives for another hour or so, Mack started the car, with a resigned sigh to his fate, and headed down the road knowing that he would go and give his report to the organization no matter the outcome and hope for the best. He drove down past where he had found the bodies of the wolves and felt a small shiver of fear run up and down his spine at the thoughts of a vamp and what they had done to the wolves in the woods.

Rounding a bend while lost in his dark thoughts, Mack

slammed the brakes of his old Honda to the floor and swerved to the right to avoid the two black SUVs that were sitting in the middle of the road. His momentum carried him toward the trees and only his quick shifter reflexes saved him from crashing into the foliage before the car came to a full stop. As the engine ticked and the dust from the road settled like a blanket over his car, Mack glanced at the two vehicles that sat blocking the way.

Mack shut down his car engine and slowly the rat shifter crawled out of the automobile and moved over to the SUVs while keeping an eye on the woods around him. He stopped a few feet from the back of the vehicles and sniffed the air as a soft breeze brought a particular smell to his nostrils. His nose wrinkled and his heart climbed up into his throat as he remembered the last time he had encountered this odor. He had stumbled on fresh vamp kill, not a very pretty sight, he thought, the memory still fresh in his mind after all these years.

Not wanting to look at what he knew he would find in the SUVs, the shifter's feet moved of their own accord as his mind silently screamed at him to turn around and run for his car and leave the area. Stopping at the open doors, the quietness and beauty of the surrounding woods only emphasized the two dried up husks that once had been wolf enforcers.

"Oh damn," Mack whispered as he moved over to the other vehicle to see if the other wolves had met the same fate, though the smell that drifted from the SUV told him that they had. Mack glanced around the woods again as something in the undergrowth moved causing him to flinch and give a small yell.

As his heart once more came back to as normal a rhythm as it would in this situation, Mack glanced inside the SUV with a grimace. Before him sat Joseph or at least what was left of him with another shifter sitting across from him in the driver's seat, both looking like some old pictures of Egyptian mummies. The skin of the shifters was dried up and pulled close to the bone and muscle of the bodies, while their lips were bared and shriveled exposing the canines in a permanent snarl in death, but the worst was the empty eye sockets that stared into the sunny morning air.

"Oh great, I guess my information was right after all. There is at least one vamp in the area and an old one by the looks of it," Mack mumbled out loud and then started at the laugh and a cheerful voice behind him.

"Very good dude, you got it in one."

Mack slowly turned around now knowing that he didn't need to worry about how he would die once he got back to the organization because he was already a dead shifter walking with this vamp here.

OOOOO

We all sat there in the silence of the cave with just the sound of Shane's crunching which, by the way, was starting to drive me crazy. The old man got up and walked over to the stove and poured himself another cup of coffee. His slow shuffle back to the table and the noise from the fae's side of the room finally got to me as I snapped, "Okay will someone please tell me what in the hell is going on?"

The crunching stopped for a few seconds as the old man sat down but then resumed as he settled back into his chair once more. "Okay, young lady, I'll tell you even though your mother should have advised you long before you hit eighteen about the real world."

"Yeah, well, she didn't, probably to protect me as she always seemed to be doing."

"Fine then, the fae there told me last night that she enlightened you that there are more than just humans in the world, right?"

"Yeah I guess, but it seems a little hard to swallow, I mean . . ."

The old man held up his hand and looked at me with a small smile. "You turning into a wolf hybrid last night, that didn't convince you?"

"Fine okay so there are shifters and fae, alright. Doesn't mean that there are really vamps out there waiting to drink my blood, old man."

Both of my companions laughed out loud and then sobered up real quick at my outburst. "You wish vamps drank blood, Ruby Red," Shane said as she hopped off the bunk and took her plate over to the counter and threw it with the other dirty dishes.

The old man looked a little annoyed as Shane hopped up on the counter and planted her butt next to the dishes. "You do know there is another chair here fae, don't you? And that those dishes won't clean themselves?"

Shane glanced at the chair, the dishes, and then at the old man and shrugged her shoulders, "Yeah and your point being, old man?"

He looked at her for a few seconds and then sighed and turned back to me with a slight shake of his head. "Okay, young lady, the way the real world works is that at the beginning there were humans and then there were us, the Supernaturals: the fae, different types of shifters, dragons, and such.

"And vamps? They were one of these 'Supernaturals', old man?"

"No, but I will get to that. We, I mean the Supernaturals that is, lived a long life, but bred slowly. Whereas the humans had a much shorter lifespan, but because of that they bred fast and multiplied like rabbits. Anyways the fae and shifters moved away from humans as their population grew, but in time they basically took over all the land masses on this planet and we had no choice but to interact with them.

From time to time, of course, there would be an . . .

accident where humans would be killed or hunted and that's where the vamps came into the equation."

I looked at the two sitting before me. "Yeah, 'accidents'," I said with a slight touch of sarcasm ringing in my voice.

Shane hopped off the counter and paced in front of me while her hair turned bright red in anger. "Yeah well these accidents weren't all one-sided, Ruby Red. Remember you're not human, you're one of us."

I glanced at the fae and then looked back at the old man. "Okay so there was killing on both sides, so then what?"

The old man glanced at Shane and then back at me. "Then we decided that humans were too dangerous to us so we, I mean the Council, decided that humans couldn't be left to live if they weren't properly ruled by us."

"Yeah right and the humans let you do this without putting up a fight?"

"Actually that was the easy part," Shane interjected with a loud laugh.

I gave a confused look as the old man chuckled along with the fae. "Yeah back then all we did was find the right humans that would sell their soul to be 'in charge' of the others of their kind and basically took over."

"You're kidding," I questioned the two and then sat there thinking over our world history and how it always seemed that the people on this planet were willing to be lead by a few. I turned back to the old shifter and shook my head at these thoughts. "Okay and the vamps?"

The old man squirmed a little and the fae looked off into the past. "Yes, the vamps. Well, it seems that some humans, a very small percentage of them have this little quirk that causes them to change into a vamp when they reach eighteen."

"Oh, sort of like what I went through then."

"Yeah, sort of like that except for humans that turn into vamps they become parasites and prey on the Supernaturals and their own kind alike".

"Oh, I see. So what, our blood tastes better to them or something?"

The old man shook his head and then looked at me with a small evil smile. "Vamps don't drink blood; they take your life force or your energy."

"Oh," was all I could get out thinking that wasn't so bad.

Shane looked at me and matched the evil little grin that the old man had. "Go ahead and tell her what happens when a vamp takes your life force."

He glanced at the fae and then looked back at me. "When a vamp takes the life force from a human, they turn that human into a sort of zombie. The human is, for all intents and purposes, dead and must do whatever the vamp commands."

"You mean a zombie like one that eats brains and all, that kind of zombie?" I gave a little laugh that died a quick death as I saw I was the only one laughing. "Oh, okay and what about us?"

"Well when a vamp drains a shifter, it leaves a dried husk behind. And when it does a fae . . ." the old man glanced at Shane.

"We just fade into nothing," the fae said with a small shudder.

"And me, what would happen to me?"

The old man gave me a peculiar look and shrugged his shoulders. "That is a good question. As I said before there never has been a hybrid like you so no one knows what would happen if you were attacked by a vamp. Maybe dry up and then disappear into nothing?"

Oh great, I thought, nothing like being one of a kind and having no one know what that kind is. Then a thought flashed through my brain and I looked at the two once more and asked, "Okay well if we control humans then why do we allow them to fight. You know wars and such garbage. Surely that hurts us too."

Once more I looked on at those grins of theirs and I had an inkling that I wasn't going to like their answer. "The wars are fights between different factions within the shifters or fae or against each other. They just use humans to fight their battles for the most part since there is so many of them. And of course there is, you know, population control," the old man said.

"Right so World War I and World War II, and Vietnam . . ."

"Yes and the Civil War here and all wars large and small are basically fights between factions of races or between the Super races themselves. In fact, your mother was the reason for the Cold War."

I stared at the two now knowing that they had got to be pulling my leg with this crap. But the more I looked at them the more I saw that they were serious about the whole thing. "Okay I'll bite, how could my mother have caused the Cold War when she was probably not even born yet? I mean she couldn't have been more than thirty-four or thirty-five tops."

Shane shook her head and gave a small laugh. "Your mother was over a hundred and fifteen years old, Ruby Red. Besides fae having a long life, we don't age in appearance until we actually pass on."

I closed my mouth where it had fallen on my chest and looked at the two once more and shook my head trying to absorb everything that they were telling me. The old man started talking once more. "Your mother was over here in this country as a diplomat after World War II when she disappeared. No one knew what had happened to her and, as she was the princess to the largest fae faction and heir to their throne, it caused quite a ruckus around the world."

"So when she got away from my father why didn't she go back home?" I whispered fearing the answer.

The old man once more looked at Shane who stopped her pacing and stared at me. "We think because by that time she was pregnant and she knew that her mother would force her to get rid of the child."

"Nice lady, my grandmother, can't wait to meet her," I said as the thought that the child she would have gotten rid of was me.

The fae smiled again which seemed to piss me off after hearing that my own grandmother wouldn't have wanted me around. "Well, Ruby Red, the queen has never been known for her niceness. In fact, she is known to be one of the most ruthless bitches in the world. No offense, old man."

The old man laughed and shook his head. "Why would I take offense to that? I'm a cat, not some mutt."

Oh great, not only do I have what I take is a psycho for a father, I have a grandmother that may be even worse. Nice family I was brought into. No wonder my mother went through all the trouble she did to keep me hidden and trained me to fight. "So then what are you doing here if my mother was afraid to go home?" I asked.

"I'm here because I was one of the only ones that really knew what had happened to your mother. When she escaped from your father, she found me and made me promise to keep your birth quiet so that neither your father nor your grandmother would ever come after you."

I stood up and started to do a little pacing of my own as the fae hopped back up on the counter top which once more generated a look of annoyance on the old man's face. "Yeah well I think that plan sort of backfired since we have been running and hiding for as long as I can remember."

A mournful look crossed Shane's face and I could swear I saw her eyes glisten with a shimmer of tears as I moved back and forth in front of her. "I'm sorry about that, Ruby Red. Your mother was my only true friend and if I could have saved her the other night I would have. I don't know how your father found out about you, but. . ."

"The rat," the old man whispered.

I stopped moving and stood there looking down at him as Shane hopped off of the counter. "What was that old man? What rat?" I said looking around the floor of the cave.

The old man looked up from his chair. "I said that your father probably found out about you with the help of the rat. He is a shifter that your father uses to locate people or information. I would say that is how he found out where your mother was each time you had to run and also about you."

"Wait. Are you telling me there are rat shifters . . ." The old man gave me an amused smile.

"Okay never mind that, so we figure this rat is the one that told my father about me so when I meet this rat, whatever his name is . . ."

"It's Mack, young lady. Mack the rat."

I stopped and looked at the old man and thought 'Mack the rat'? Really? I then gave him a promise I hoped to keep. "Fine when I find Mack the rat he and I are going to have a long and interesting talk, and I by interesting I mean it is going to be very painful for him."

Both the old man and the fae were quiet at my statement and the only sound I heard was a tiny dripping of liquid. I looked down at the drops of blood leaking onto the floor from my clenched fists. Slowly opening them, I saw that in my anger my claws had extended and punctured the palms of my hands, but the blood stopped flowing as soon as my hands opened and my claws retracted and a few seconds later the wounds healed as if they had never happened.

"Well I guess that's one thing that is true, that werewolves heal fast," I said with a small laugh showing my hands to my two companions.

Both were silent as they walked over and took my hands and examined the wounds that were no longer there. Hell, there wasn't even any scarring from the punctures. The old man went white under his tanned hide while Shane backed off from me with a frightened look in her eyes. "What's wrong now guys? I thought werewolves were supposed to have great healing powers."

The old man dropped my hand like it was on fire then glanced over at the fae. "You want to tell her or should I?"

"Tell me what? What is wrong with the two of you?"

As I stood staring at the two of them as I heard a small pop behind me, and caught the slightest whiff of smoke as a rough gravelly voice said, "Well, tootsie, they're afraid because only vamps have the power to heal that fast with no scarring."

# PERCY

Mack turned slowly around and looked at his worst fear. The thought, 'that's a vamp', flashing through his mind as he took in the person standing before him. He stared at the long blond hair and blue eyes of the teenager dressed in old board shorts and a Led Zepplin shirt, which had seen better days, and smiled.

The teen smiled back, showing his long fangs. Then the blue of his eyes faded to a dead white, the cheeks sunk in making the young face thinner and more skull-like wiping the smile right off Mack's face. "What's the matter, dude? You act like you've seen a ghost or maybe a vamp?" the teen whispered with a mad giggle as he slinked toward the shifter.

Mack froze, partly in fright, partly because he knew that it would be useless to run from the monster in front of him. For no matter how fast a shifter was they were still no match for the speed of one of these creatures. The vamp slowly circled the shifter and once more came eye to eye with Mack. "Very good, shifter; most of your kind would have run or tried to fight like your friends there," the vamp said pointing over Mack's shoulder at the two black SUVs. "By the way, what kind of shifter are you? You don't smell like a wolf."

"I'm a rat," Mack replied in a respectful whisper. There was no reason to piss off the vamp and die any earlier than necessary.

"Yeah okay, dude, just never smelled one of you before," the vamp said with a sniff. Then, as Mack watched, the vamp's eyes turned the deep blue of the ocean and his fangs retracted giving the vamp back his surfer boy good looks once more.

Mack looked into those eyes and figured he had nothing to lose since he was going to die anyway so he whispered to the vamp, "Those aren't my friends, by the way."

The vamp's smile got bigger and then he walked past Mack and back to the vehicles. "Yeah dude, no problem. Just used that as a figure of speech, I figured you weren't buddy-buddy when I saw how they treated you before," the vamp said as he grabbed what was left of Joseph and pulled him out of the SUV and tossed the body over the shifter's head. The vamp hopped up into the seat and looked at Mack as he slowly turned to face him.

"So you'll let me go?" Mack asked as hope briefly flared in his heart that he would walk away from this encounter with the one boogie man that all shifters feared.

But that hope died at the vamp's next words. "Yeah well now that does present me with a little problem, dude."

Mack gulped back his breakfast, which was threatening to rise up out of his stomach and looked at the vamp wishing that he could have seen at least one more sunset. "And what is that problem, Mr. . ."

The vamp hopped out of the SUV and in a flash was standing next to Mack with his arms around the shifter's shoulders. "It's Davey, rat. The name is Davey, no Mr., just Davey."

In his fright, a small laugh escaped the shifter's lips and then was stifled as quickly as it came up. Mack tried to stammer an apology to the vamp. The vamp cut him off with a laugh of his own. "Hey dude, no worries. I know, right? A vamp named Davey, but you know how it is? What can you do? It's the name that my parents gave me." The vamp's laugh stopped and once more his eyes turned white, like a three day old dead fish, and his fangs extended. "Of course, they didn't think it was funny when I fed them to some of my pets. But hey, what can you do, right dude? I mean you sometimes just need to punish people when they screw up, am I right or what?"

"Yeah right, Mr., I mean Davey, sure nothing you could do," Mack stammered.

"I mean Davey just isn't a vamp's name. I mean it should have been something like Aramastus, or Aleron, or maybe even Jedediah, but no they have to go and name me Davey.

Can you believe that someone would do that to their kid?" the vamp rambled on.

Mack nodded as the vamp rattled on and thought that this was not only a vamp standing next to him, but it was one bat-shit crazy vamp at that. Though the shifter focused back to what the vamp was saying at his next words. "But enough about my name, let's go back to the problem I have right now, rat. You see the problem is, is that I just don't like shifters. Now don't take this personal or anything. It's not just you I don't like, but all shifters in general. Plus I have to find this one girl and all, well like I said nothing personal dude, so when I kill you, you will understand that right?"

"Girl? Do you mean the hybrid girl?"

The vamp stopped dead in his tracks, his hand tightening and digging into Mack's shoulder and bringing a small whimper of pain from the shifter. "Just what do you know about this girl, rat? Do you know where she is?"

Mack's mind was working overtime, thinking that his next words could get him killed or could save his life for at least another few minutes. "I was looking for her here in Bellingham. I don't know exactly where she is, but I know that I can find her for you, Davey."

The vamp turned Mack so that once more they were looking eye to eye. The shifter was hypnotized by the stare of the vamp's dead fish eyes that so contrasted with the rest of the surfer boy look that he wore before. "Why were you looking for this particular girl, rat?"

Once more Mack felt like he was skating on the sharp edge of a knife and wasn't sure which answer would keep himself from being killed by this creature. He couldn't tear his eyes off of the vamp and threw the dice, hoping whichever way they landed his death would be quick but had little hope of that happening. "Her father, Marcus, has been looking for her. That's his enforcers that you took out there in the SUVs."

The creature's eyes seem to tear down into the shifter's soul, opening it up for the vamp to examine. After a few seconds, the vamp's hand released its pressure on Mack's shoulder as a big smile lit up his face. "Guess what, dude? It's your lucky day."

"Oh?"

"Oh yes, rat, it's your lucky day because you are now working for me." With that, the vamp seized him in an iron grip and sunk his fangs into the shifter's neck.

OOOOO

I turned in a huff to the voice that had called me 'tootsie', ready to kick some butt but stopped at the figure that stood there looking up at me. Out of all the creatures I had imagined there were in the world, a four-foot green dragon wearing shades, a bowler hat, and chomping on an unlit cigar was not one of them. I glanced back at the old man and Shane and then back at the dragon and rubbed my eyes, hoping that this figure would disappear back to where it came from.

"What's the matter, baby doll, never seen a dragon before?" the creature said as he peeked over his dark glasses at me, both eyebrows wiggling up and down on his forehead.

I gathered myself and figured what the hell if there can be werewolves, fae, and other Supernaturals in the world why not this dragon? "I haven't ever seen a dragon before and if you want anyone else to see one you will stop calling me 'tootsie' or 'baby doll'."

The dragon leaned around me and took in the other two in the cave and smiled. "I like her! She's a feisty little one, isn't she?

"Hello Percy," Shane said in a cold voice. "You here for a reason?"

Percy? Seriously? A dragon that was named Percy? Oh, this is getting better and better my mind screamed, finally hitting its overload point. I let out a laugh and turned to the fae. "You know this thing?"

"Hey watch it, girly. This 'thing' has feelings you know," the gravelly voice sounded once more behind me.

"Yes, everyone, unfortunately, knows Percy, young lady," the old man said.

"Hey kitty, still hitting the catnip?" The voice sounded behind me again, bringing forth a low growl from the old man.

I turned to the dragon and looked at him for a few seconds then sighed. "Okay, so what is a four-foot-nothing dragon doing here? And just for your information, I'm not a vamp I'm half fae and half werewolf."

"No, honey pie, you're the prophecy – that is what you are," the dragon said with a smirk written on his face.

I peeked back at the other two and saw the shock on their faces and turned back to face Percy when I heard the fae whisper something behind me. "What was that, Shane?"

"She said she forgot about that," the dragon laughed, and snickered as I heard another low growl from behind me, but this time coming from the fae.

I rubbed my forehead, trying to prevent the headache that was starting to build behind my eyes. I shook my head and thought that of all the absurd things that I had heard today this one was the worst. "Okay, shorty, tell me about this prophecy."

"Hey watch it there 'baby dol . . .'"

I stepped forward feeling my claws and fangs extend. Percy stopped whatever he was going to say and he took in the look in my eyes. "Okay, okay no names, truce?"

I stopped my advance and took a deep breath to settle myself down. "Yeah truce, as long as you behave yourself but one more of those 'cute' little names out of you and you are going to find yourself made into luggage."

"Touchy, isn't she? Just to let you know, it's alligator that you make luggage out of – not dragon," Percy said as he once more looked around me at the other two and then back at me.

I looked down at the dragon and gave him an evil little smile. "Try me and see, Percy. You look just the right size to make a purse."

Shane shrugged her shoulders and said, "The prophecy, Percy?"

"Oh yeah, the prophecy," the dragon said, ignoring my last remark. "Yeah well, a long time ago a wise dragon, wiser beyond his years and any other dragon's years . . ."

There was another low growl from the old man that stopped Percy in the middle of his lecture. "Get on with it, Percy. We all know that you're the one that made the prophecy, cut your self-serving bull, and remind us what it was."

"Oh, alright then. Damn, everyone is so touchy this morning, I . . ."

"PERCY!" the three of us shouted at the same time.

Percy stopped his grumbling and looked down at the floor. "You know, I don't need this kind of abuse. If I wanted to stand around and be shouted at I'd just go back home. I can get . . ."

I walked over to the little fellow, bent down and put my arm around his shoulders and handed him a napkin from the nearby table as I heard his small sniffles. Oh great. Now I had to babysit a dragon, I thought, as I rubbed him on the back. His green scales felt like I was rubbing my hand over granite but it was the only thing I could think to do so we could hear this damn prophecy once and for all. The dragon took the napkin and blew long and hard, filling it with green snot. As he tried to hand it back to me, I waved it away for there was no way I was going to touch that gross piece of paper.

Percy looked over the top of his glasses as he gave a final sniff at the other two watching this pathetic scene being acted out. The dragon stuck his tongue out at them, snarled, and threw the napkin over his shoulder where it made a large splat when it hit the ground. "See the cutie here . . ." Percy stopped talking as he took in the glare I was throwing his way. "I mean Ruby here knows how to be compassionate, not like you two lowly creatures."

"Yeah well if you don't remind us what that prophecy was, dragon, I'm the one who is going to make you into a set of matching luggage," Shane said as she stepped forward, drawing her swords from their resting place.

Percy held up both hands and then tried to duck behind me as the fae took another step toward him. "Okay, okay, just chill, fae, I will tell you."

"You had better, dragon, for if you keep messing around I

will get you if the fae doesn't," the cat shifter growled at Percy.

Percy shook his head at the two and then glanced at me. "Okay, the prophecy is that a young one will be born between two races. She will have the power of all creatures: shifters, fae, dragons, and even vamps. She will be born to protect all from the evil that lurks in all creature's souls."

I stood up and looked at the other two, who had these thoughtful looks on their face, and then back down at Percy. "That's it? That's the big prophecy? I thought prophecies were supposed to rhyme and such?"

"Well yeah what more do you want, Ruby? I'm a dragon, not a poet," Percy asked with a quick shrug of his shoulders.

"Well, just what am I suppose to be doing exactly? I mean protect all who, and from what evil in whose soul?"

The dragon gave a big sigh like he was being put out by my questions, but I figured that I had better nail down what I was supposed to be doing and who I was supposed being doing it against. "Listen, Ruby, it's a dragon prophecy, see we can't just come out and say what you're supposed to do. You're just, you know, supposed to go and do it," Percy said with another shrug of his shoulders and a shake of his head. "Come on you want everything in this life spelled out for you?"

I glanced over at the other two and saw that they wouldn't

be much help as they were sitting there nodding their head at everything that the dragon was saying. Oh great, I thought, I've lost my mother, my home, then I find out I'm not human I'm a half werewolf/fae, and then to top it all off now I find I'm supposed to save the downtrodden of the world, but no one has any idea how I'm to go about this. Can this day get any worse?

You know you should never ask that question when you're having a bad day because fate has a way of stepping up and slapping you in the face. A loud echoing bang came from the cave entrance and then was followed by several determined knocks on the door that bounced around the stone walls.

"You expecting any more company, old man?" I asked as the sound of the pounding became louder and more determined by the second. Whoever was outside that door really, really wanted to come and visit and I don't think they were going to take a polite 'no visitors please' from any of us.

The old man got up and slid aside a small window in the thick door, took a quick peek and then slammed the window shut. He turned to us with a look of panic and I could see that his outdoor tan had gone the way of the Dodo bird as he was as white as a ghost. Which I was hoping wasn't what was on the other side of that door, a ghost that is, come to think of it.

"Zombies," the old man whispered, and I gave out a small

laugh, that stopped as I looked at the other two and saw that they were as freaked as the old man. Just then the window busted out with a shower of splinters and a smelly putrid hand reached through it trying to grab the old man.

As the shifter moved back from the door, I looked at the gray, gnarled hand then caught a whiff of a stronger stench along with the sound of moaning coming through the window. "Please tell me you have another way out of this cave, old man," I whined bringing my hand up to my nose to cut down on the rotting smell that was now drifting into the room.

The question seemed to jog the other three out of the stupor they had fallen in and into action. The old man and Shane ran to the back of the cave and moved aside one of the bunks that lined the wall. "Yeah, sorry about that, just don't like zombies," the old man said with some embarrassment in his voice.

"No problem, just as long as we have a way to get out of here. I have no desire to have my brains eaten out by the undead or to be made one of them if you know what I mean?"

As the old man and the fae moved the bunk and gathered up some supplies in a pack, Percy looked up at me and gave me a sick little smile. "Well, you don't have to worry about that, Ruby, because only vamps can make more zombies."

"But the part the little squirt here didn't tell you about is that the zombies don't just eat your brains they eat everything and I mean everything, clothes, bones, meat, I mean when they are through there is no trace that you even existed," Shane whispered.

I think I turned a little green at that thought and felt my breakfast start to come up, but swallowed it down and glanced back at the door and saw that it wouldn't hold long under the onslaught it was taking. "But of course the worst part is that they keep you alive as long as they can while they feed. For some reason they like their meals fresh and squirming while they eat," the old man said with a wild laugh.

I glanced back at the door and then at the three once more. "Okay, I got all that so why are we standing around talking? Let's get the hell out of here," I said hearing the slight edge of panic hit my voice as I watched the other three nod their heads in agreement. The old man hit a button low on the wall and it slid sideways and we all moved into the darkness behind it. As I watched the wall sliding shut, I heard the cave door give way but the sounds of the zombies were cut off when the door's lock snapped into place as it finally shut.

# THE WALK

Mack slowly opened his eyes and looked up at the blue sky above him. He could see a lone cloud that was moving across the blue riding the winds like a rabbit flying across a field. "Sort of looks like a rabbit, dude, don't you think?" a voice sounded from his right and banged around inside his skull like a giant brass ball.

The shifter let out a low moan partly from the pain that the sound of that voice brought to his head and partly because he thought he was dead and hopefully in Heaven. Mack rolled over on his side and thought definitely not heaven as he looked at the vamp that was once more perched inside one of the SUVs; maybe Hell, but, definitely not Heaven. "Oh man what did you do to me, vamp?" he groaned while he slowly got to his feet wondering why he wasn't in the same condition as the other shifters in the trucks around him.

The vamp let out a low mocking laugh as he put his hand to his chest. "What? Me do something to you, dude? Oh, now I'm hurt. Here I go and let my newfound friend live, and you go and accuse me of doing some nasty to you dude. Really I am just shocked at the injustice of it all."

Mack stood there weaving on his unsteady feet not sure if it was better to face the vamp standing or to just give into his body's notion to hit the ground and give up on this life and end the pain and misery he was feeling. "Fine vamp, then what's wrong with me and why is it every time you talk to me it feels like I got a cannon ball ping-ponging inside my head?"

"Well that's an easy one, dude," Davey said as he hopped out of the vehicle and walked over to the shifter. "It's a little-known fact that when a vamp bites a Supernatural and only takes a little bit of its energy, that creature then falls under the control of the vamp that bit it."

Mack quickly straightened up at that news, bringing a fresh new level of pain to his body and eliciting another moan at the excruciating feeling. "You mean I'm one of your zombies? I thought you could only do that to humans."

Davey patted the shifter's shoulder in mock comfort making Mack stagger from the weight and bringing another groan from the rat. "Oh of course not, dude. A Supernatural can never be turned into one of my pets, only a human can, but I found out a long time ago that if I take a small amount of your energy into me and transfer some of mine into you then I can see, hear, and feel everything you can along with the benefit of you having to obey my commands."

Mack raised his head and looked at the creature with horror written on his face. "Please tell me you're kidding me, vamp."

The vamp's eyes turned again and the shifter felt himself flying through the air with no conscious idea of how that had happened. The SUV he hit rocked back and forth and he could feel and hear something crack as he met the immobile object. God hopefully that kills me and takes me out of this nightmare, the shifter thought as the edges of his vision started to go black. Hearing a crunch of gravel in front of him, the shifter blinked his eyes a few times and saw that the blackness that threatened to engulf him was fading. There in front of him kneeled the vamp with his eyes now the color of blue and a wide smile plastered across his face. "Oh, and by the way, dude, you also get my quick healing powers so you're not going to die just quite yet."

Sure enough, as Mack shifted around on the ground he could feel his body repairing itself in seconds which would take a normal shifter minutes or maybe even hours to do. Hell, even the voice that sounded in his head was down to a dull roar and at least tolerable. "So why did you do this to me?"

The vamp's smile got wider and he leaned in closer to Mack and whispered, "Why dude, because we are bros now, and I want you to do me a little favor."

Mack looked up into the creature's eyes and knew that he was not going to like the answer but asked anyway. "What favor?

"Well dude, I want you to call your boss and tell him that he needs to come up here to Bellingham and save his daughter from the terrible monster that is stalking her."

Mack shook his head as though trying to clear the voice in his head that was reinforcing the vamp's words, but he could feel the compulsion to follow the vamp's instructions grow as Davey's eyes bore into his. "Don't even think of fighting it, dude. I have complete control over you, and I will know if you don't follow my orders to the letter."

The shifter gave up what little resistance he had and as he relaxed and leaned back against the SUV behind him, he could feel the last little niggling pain in his body and head disappear. Davey stood and reached down with his hand to help the shifter to his feet as he chuckled, "There see now isn't that better when you don't fight your new master, shifter?" Mack took the offered hand and stood up and nodded at the vamp. "Good then. Now be a good shifter and go back to town and do as I told you, and maybe after all this is over we'll go our separate ways."

The rat shifter let go of the icy cold hand of the vamp and walked to his car, digging the keys out of his pocket that somehow had managed to stay in there even after all the abuse that he had suffered at the hands of the vamp. As he climbed into the car, he hesitated and then looked back at the vamp. "I do have one question, Davey, if I may?"

The vamp once more moved in a flash and suddenly his frowning face was just inches in front of the shifter looking him in the eye. "Why certainly, dude, we're bros. Remember? Friends can ask friends anything."

Mack took a deep gulp of air instantly regretting his curiosity. "Yeah. Well, why are you so interested in this girl?"

Davey's frown faded and the wide smile showed once more as the blue eyes sparkled with his merriment. "Oh, why that is an easy question to answer, dude. I need to keep my one true love safe from all the riffraff in this evil world."

Mack stared in those mad eyes and nodded at the vamp, then he stepped back the few inches that his car allowed as the eyes turned all white and the vamp's fangs extended. "Now I would suggest, dude, that you stop asking questions and go do what your master told you to do. Or bros or not . . ."

Mack moved as fast as he could, collapsing into his car and slamming the door. Jamming the keys into the ignition and with a flick of his wrist, he had the car running and moving once more down the road toward town. As he looked up into the rearview mirror all Mack could see behind him was empty road. The thought flashed through his mind that he should really now consider heading to the Canadian border if he wanted to live through this ordeal, but the thought died as a quiet growl in his head sounded causing a sharp stab of pain behind his eyes. Then a small nasty voice whispered in his head, "Don't even think it, dude."

OOOOO

I heard a small click and watched as the flashlight that the old man was holding in his hand lit up the dark of the tunnel. I have never liked enclosed spaces and with the four of us standing around just behind the door that led into the cave there wasn't much room to move. "Now what?" I asked a hint of panic still in my voice.

The old man flashed the light down the tunnel and gave me a wink. "Now young lady we go down this little tunnel and get away from the creatures that invaded my home."

I looked back at the wall surprised that we couldn't hear the creatures behind it when I heard a small chuckle from the old man. "Don't worry, dear, it's reinforced steel. Nothing is getting through there at least for awhile anyways. Now let's all just take a quick stroll down this way," the old man said as he headed down the semi-dark hole in the ground.

We walked about a hundred feet down the tunnel when the old man stopped and pointed the light at the ground where a white mark was painted. "Okay now for a little house cleaning," he said giving a nasty little laugh as he opened a panel in the wall and pushed one button then a second.

Through the ground I could feel a low rumble, a small puff of air then the slight presence of dust and dirt filled the air.

"What was that?" I asked.

"Oh, that was my home and the cave that we were in. I had them wired for just this kind of emergency."

"Wired? Wired with what?" a little more panic seeping into my voice.

A great big smile lit up the old man's face. "Why it was wired with enough explosives to leave nothing of my house or the cave that we were in. I expect that the vamp that is around here will need to make some new zombies since the ones that were back there are in little itty bitty pieces or flat as a pancake under a ton of rock."

I caught the other two nodding at the old man's words before they all turned and started walking down the dark tunnel. I took one long look behind me as the little bit of dust settled onto the ground, turned and followed them into the dark.

OOOOO

I don't know how long we were walking, but with only the old man's light to keep back the dark it seemed like we had been on the move for hours. As we moved down the tunnel, I could hear Percy mumbling to himself about how unappreciated dragons were and how he had never said anything about vamps or zombies when he had made his prophecy. His nonstop chatter was the only sound in the tunnel, even though every once in while I thought I heard a small sound behind us like cloth scraping on rock. But since none of the others seemed to have noticed anything I just put it down to my overactive imagination.

After what seemed like hours the tunnel opened up into a small cave that had a dark pool of water to one side. As the old man shone the light around I could see that the area around us wasn't much bigger than the cave we had left, but it lacked the amenities that the other one had, such as food or bunks or a toilet. "So are we there yet?" I whined.

Everyone turned to look at me with that look of 'really' written across their faces. "Sorry," I mumbled. "Guess I'm a still a little tired from last night's change, and I need to use the restroom."

Percy shook his head, while the fae didn't say a word, but just walked off and sat down on a rock with her back to us. The old man shone the light around once more then walked over to another pile of rocks and set the pack down and then started to root around deep within it. After a few seconds, he came up with a canteen and tossed it over to me with a low growl. "Restroom is in that dark corner over there and before you come back here, young lady, go and fill this over at that waterhole."

I caught the canteen and was about ready to toss it back with a quick quip on what he could do with the canteen when I caught the look on his face and decided that maybe it would be better if I just go and do what he said. "Fine, but how about some light to see what I'm doing?"

The old man gave another growl and pointed at the pool.

"Just go do it, young lady. It's not like there is anything down here that can hurt you."

I went over to the corner that the old man had pointed to and relieved myself from a full bladder then stomped over to the water in a huff, wondering why the fae or the dragon couldn't have gotten the canteen filled since I was supposed to be the big savior of the Supernatural world. I was stopped by that slight scraping sound again. I turned and looked around the area, but for the most part, pretty much all of the cave was hidden in shadow. "Hey, old man are you sure there . . ." I said turning to look back at the other three when I felt an icy cold hand clamp itself around my arm.

I let out a scream while turning and glancing at whatever had a hold of me. As I came around, the canteen connected with someone's head. I heard the sound like a cracking egg and watched it loll to the side of its body and almost touch its shoulder. From the decay and smell coming from the body, I figured that somehow a zombie had escaped the old man's fireworks.

The eyes of the creature blinked and instead of letting go of me, its grip just tightened on my arm. Without conscious thought, I dropped the canteen and reached over with my other hand grabbed the creature's hair and gave a quick jerk. The ripping sound that echoed throughout the darkness of the cave drowned out the sound of disgust I moaned as I realized that I held the creature's head in my hand. Its eyes were still blinking at me, its teeth snapping, while its body walked around the cave like a chicken without its head. If this situation wasn't so serious I would have laughed. The body was wandering around waving its hands in the air looking for the head that I held.

Of course, I did the only thing I could think of and dropped the head as I heard a noise behind me. Turning I could see the other three standing there glancing at the creature then at me. Percy stepped forward and patted me on the arm as he looked down at the zombie. "Pretty good reflexes there, Ruby."

I looked down at the dragon then at the other two. "That is a zombie, right?" I said as the body of the creature was now on its hands and knees feeling around on the ground for its head. Like I said before it would have been funny if I hadn't known what the creature was capable of.

Shane stepped forward and drew one of her swords and pinned the zombie's body to the ground just inches from its head, but I could see the hands reach out and I nudged the head further away from it but being careful to keep the gnashing teeth away from my toes. "Yes, Ruby Red, that is a zombie."

I looked down at the blinking eyes and the body that was desperately trying to get to its head and then up at my companions. "I thought all you had to do to kill these things was to destroy its head? Why's it still moving around like that?"

Percy stepped up to the zombie's head and, grabbing it by

the hair, held it aloft in his hands. "Lesson one, baby . . . I mean Ruby is that must totally destroy the head of the zombie like this," as the dragon breathed fire out of his mouth and the head turned to ash.

"Oh man that is seriously creepy, you guys," I said as Shane pulled the sword from the body and I watched it disintegrate into a big pool of goo. "

"Okay that seems simple enough, I guess," I said then looked at the old man who hadn't said a word so far. "And you, I thought you said there wasn't anything down here that could hurt me."

The old man smiled and shook his head at my temper tantrum. "Did it hurt you, young lady?"

"Well, no."

The old man's smile got bigger. "Okay, then what's the problem?"

"Well, that's not the point, I . . . wait a minute did you guys know that this thing was down here? Was it following us from the old man's cave?"

Percy looked down at the ground, a guilty look written on his face and when I looked up at the other two I could see the truth written across theirs. "You did, didn't you? You guys knew that this thing was following us. That's what that sound was that I heard in the dark, wasn't it?"

Shane stood there looking at me with a frown. Percy kept

looking at the ground as the old man walked over and put his arm on my shoulder. "Listen, young lady, you were never in any real danger with us here. We had to find out if you would go through the change under stress or . . ."

"Use magic," Shane said. "But she didn't do any of that so that prophecy thingy is just like the rest of that dragon, full of hot air," the fae said as she pointed at Percy then sniffed the air and walked back to the rock she had been sitting on earlier.

The old man gave my shoulder a quick squeeze and then reached down and took the canteen from my hand and started down to the pool of the water. "You two go back and get some rest, young lady, and I'll get the water."

Of course, you will now that there aren't any more zombies down here, I thought as I moved over to where the old man had left his pack and sat down against one of the rocks. "There aren't any more zombies down here right?" I said into the dark cave not getting an answer to my question but a small laugh from the old man.

Percy came walking over and perched himself on another rock across from me. "I just want to say sorry, Ruby, about not telling you about the zombie, but we needed to see what you would do with your powers."

I watched as the old man walked up from the water and dug through his pack and produced four cups out of its depths. As he poured some powder into the cups and then the water, I glanced back at Percy the anger coming out in my voice. "Listen, dragon, I have no idea what powers you guys think I have, but I just found out about this crazy stuff a couple of days ago. I am out of my league running around having zombies, shifters, and a vamp chasing me all over the place."

The dragon listened to me without a word until my rant was done then his face lit up with a smile."Yes well, Ruby that is why your mother brought you here. She knew that you would need help learning your potential. The kitty over there," a small growl came from where the old man stood, "helped you with the change, and the fae there will help you with her kind of magic . . ."

"And you, dragon?"

"Why me, I'm here to teach you the most important thing – how to do dragon fire magic." This elicited a snicker from the other two.

"You mean what you did with that zombie's head," I said ignoring the two creatures in the dark.

Percy looked a little crestfallen and then stared at the ground. "Yes sort of like that, but more powerful."

"Okay, but . . ." I was going to ask more, but about then the old man called us over to where he was standing. Percy hopped up from his perch and shot over to the old man. I slowly climbed to my feet and moved over to the two of them wishing for the thousandth time that I was back at home with my mother and had no idea or thoughts about

Supernaturals.

The old man passed me one of the cups that he had been working on and another to Shane as she walked up to our little group. "It's not much, but it will keep us alive until we get where we are going," the old man said slamming the drought down his throat and then giving a loud belch. "Oh yeah, that's the good stuff."

I took a quick sniff at the cup then almost dropped it as I thought that the zombie I had fought not too long ago smelled better than this concoction. I started to hand my full cup back to the old man. "No thanks, I'm still full from this morning."

The old man looked at the cup then at me and snarled, "Drink it, young lady, or I'll make you drink."

I took a deep breath and slammed the drink down in a gulp. For a second my throat refused to swallow, but then it did and the liquid in my mouth hit my stomach with a blast. I felt the heat that was rolling in my middle reach out to other parts of my body and then I felt a renewed energy surge throughout me.

"Now that wasn't so bad was it, young lady?" the old man smirked.

I sputtered a little then shook my head as I handed back the empty cup. "Yeah not bad at all, old man, as long as you like drinking lighter fluid."

The old man gave a small chuckle then turned to Shane

who just looked at me with a smirk and slowly drank the nasty drink down. "Not bad, old man, but a little tame for the fae," she said as she handed the cup to him.

I looked over at the dragon who was holding his empty cup out with a smile to the old man."Got any more?"

I just turned away whispering under my breath. "Suck-ups," I said as I went back to my rock. I could hear both the old man and Shane laughing as the dragon kept asking them what was so funny.

I sat down and leaned my head back and closed my eyes to take a short rest when I felt a hand on my shoulder. "Ruby Red, it is time to go now," Shane's voice whispered in the now dark cave.

I looked around, my eyes now adjusted to the dark and could see the old man and the dragon standing at the other end of the cave opening leading wherever we were headed for. "What, why is the light out, I . . ."

"Not to worry, Ruby Red, you took a little nap and we turned out the light so you could have your sleep undisturbed."

I struggled a little getting up while looking at my three companions. "Sorry about that, guys, I . . ." I muttered sleepily.

The old man waved away my apologies and turned on the flashlight once more. "No problem, young lady, after the first change most shifters take a little while to get their energy fully back, but that little drink I gave you should help."

I stretched out a little as the old man told me that we would be at the end of the tunnel in a few hours and that Shane had backtracked to make sure that we wouldn't have any more undead behind us. I nodded at the fae as we started once more down the dark hole that was lit only by the old man's dim light.

# THE GATHERING

Mack waited in the parking lot of Bellingham International Airport and chuckled to himself as he looked at the small building that housed the airport services, but the laughter died as he watched the organization's private jet come in for a landing.

The rat shifter straightened up a few minutes later as he watched Marcus and four of the biggest enforcers he had ever seen move across the parking lot toward where he stood waiting. As the leader of the organization got closer to his informant, Mack's eyes dropped to the ground to avoid looking into the leader's eyes.

Marcus stopped, looking the smaller shifter up and down, growling, "Keys, rat."

He held out the hand holding the keys to the two black SUVs that he had rented for the leader's use while he was in town. One of the giants standing behind Marcus took the keys and without a word moved off toward the vehicles. Mack glanced up at Marcus and asked, "Is this muscle all you brought, sir?"

Marcus stared at the rat for a few seconds, some niggling little feeling bouncing in his head that something seemed to be off with this insignificant shifter, but he couldn't for the life of him figure out what it was. The leader shook the thought away and then watched as two more enforcers moved out of the airport building hauling the group's luggage. "Not that it is any of your concern, rat, but no this isn't everyone I have coming up from Seattle. I have four more crews driving up right now. They should be in this hick town in an hour or so at the most and then we can finally clear up this little problem."

Mack gave a quick little snort so low that the shifters standing around him were not sure that they had heard the noise at all. The rat quickly looked down at the ground and gave a little cough to cover his mistake as Marcus once more stared daggers at the rat. Yeah, something was up with this creature and the wolf was once again feeling that little warning of danger pinging his senses. "So rat, how did you find out about this vamp that is after my daughter anyways?"

Mack hesitated for just a second looking as though he was listening to some inner voice when a smile crossed his face. "Oh just some informers that live in this town know about the vamp and some others found your crew's bodies, sir. So I just put two and two together and figured that well you know . . ."

Marcus waved his hand to cut off the shifter's monologue and stepped closer to the rat. "There is something different about you, Mack. I don't know what it is, but if I find that you are in any way connected with the destruction of my crews you will wish for a quick death when I'm through with you. Do you understand me, rat?"

Mack looked up, his eyes having an eerie light to them that Marcus put off to the late afternoon's sun. "Oh, of course, sir, I understand perfectly. Like I said though when we talked earlier I have some very good sources in this town, and . . ."

Mack was interrupted as one of the enforcers walked up from the vehicles and bumped him aside. "The bags are in the trucks, sir, and we are ready to go."

"And the other crews?" Marcus asked his man.

The shifter threw a glance at Mack then looked back at his leader before answering, not liking the thought of talking organization business in front of the creature. "They will be up here in an hour and will meet us at the Bellwether Hotel."

"Alright then let's go get checked in," Marcus said as the group of enforcers around him headed toward the black SUVs they were using to get around town. As they reached the truck, one of his men opened the door but before Marcus crawled into it, he looked back at the rat shifter and bellowed, "And you, rat, I want you to spend the next hour out in this little pissant town and find out for me exactly where this vamp is hiding, got that?"

Mack nodded his head at the wolf as Marcus smiled to see that no matter what he thought was wrong with the rat he seemed to still take orders like he should. "Good rat," Marcus whispered then climbed inside the truck and settled himself down for the short ride to the hotel.

Mack watched the SUVs move off toward town. After a few seconds a dazed look came over his face then it disappeared as fast as it came. With a sly smile crossing his face, the shifter nodded at the empty air around him as he whispered, "Yes master." Then he climbed into his beat-up old Honda and headed away from the airport himself.

Marcus looked out the window at the small town as the SUVs moved toward the hotel; his mind a thousand miles away as his conversation with the rat shifter played through his thoughts. "Something wrong, sir?" one of the enforcers from the front seat asked.

The leader of the organization startled for an instant and glared at the other shifter causing him to drop his eyes from Marcus's. The shifter glanced up from up under his brows and stammered, "Sir, we just, well you know . . ."

Marcus let out a small growl then leaned forward and tapped the enforcer on the shoulders. "It's fine, Samuel, you are just doing your job."

The enforcer glanced up at his leader then down again. "Was it the rat, sir? Something seemed off with that creature."

Marcus nodded his head at the muscle that was there to protect him and smiled at the thought. He had handpicked all his personal enforcers for their size but made sure that they were smart enough to also keep him alive. "Yeah it was the rat and something was a little off with him. When we get to the hotel call up more enforcers from Seattle; I want to flood this town with bodies so we find this vamp and my daughter."

Samuel nodded and pulled out a small book and started to write inside as the SUVs pulled up to the Bellwether Hotel. Two shifters from Bellingham started to move toward their leader's vehicle but were pushed out of the way as the Seattle shifters exited from the first truck and surrounded Marcus's SUV. The leader exited the vehicle with his entourage never once acknowledging the local shifters and entered the posh hotel.

OOOOO

As we moved through the dimly lit tunnel I was mostly lost in my own thoughts as I half-listened to the arguing and grumbling of the three in front of me. It seemed that the fae and the old man were questioning the prophecy of the dragon and whether or not I was the true child named in it when something caused me to stop in midstride. "What was that about dinosaurs, Shane?"

The other three with me stopped and turned to look back. The old man laughed loudly and Percy stared at the ground, a deep frown crossing his face. The fae walked back to me, her face lit up with a sly little smile of her own. "I said that this dragon here, Ruby Red, does not have the best of track records with his prophecies considering it is his fault that the dinosaurs got wiped off the face of this world."

I glanced over at the old man who was by now nearly bent over double with laughter and then at the dragon. "Well, Percy?"

Percy kicked a small pebble and looked at the other two in annoyance. "It wasn't my fault that the dumb dragons mistook my words and started that war."

I shook my head at the dragon, figuring I wasn't going to get anything more out of him and looked back at the fae. "I don't get it. What does he have to do with the dinosaurs?"

Shane sat down on a boulder as if settling in for a long story. "Well, see it is like this, Ruby Red. The English dragons are the longest living creatures in this world. In fact, the few dragons that are still around were here when the dinosaurs roamed the earth. From what we have gathered all was going along just fine when Percy here made a little prophecy that caused a war among the dragons and all but wiped out life as they knew it in this world. It wasn't a meteorite that killed off the dinosaurs, but this little creature here," the fae said with a casual flip of her hand in Percy's direction.

As the dragon marched over to where the fae sat, I saw the

tunnel light up from the flames that engulfed his face and watched as steam issued from his ears. "I'll have you know, fae, that things have been gravely blown out of proportion about what happened back then. I was . . ."

"Okay, then how about Pompeii, dragon? Or what was that, oh yeah, the Civil War in this country? Then there was World War II, dragon," the old man whispered as he had stopped laughing and was now leaning against the wall of the tunnel. "This, of course, brought your mother to this country, young lady, which, by the way, started the whole Cold War incident."

The dragon turned in the direction of the old man, one hand resting on his forehead and the other waving in the air as though he could wipe the old man's words from the heavens above. "No, no, no those were not my fault, really. What I told those little idiots was . . . see it's just that no one listens, Ruby Red," the dragon whined turning to look at me his big eyes once more looking like they were ready to fill with tears.

I moved over to the dragon and laid my hand on his shoulder. "Is what they are saying true, Percy? I thought you said most of those were fights between different factions?" I questioned the other two.

The old man nodded at my question and then pointed at the dragon who was standing there pouting. "They were fights between factions all caused by some prophecy from him."

The dragon turned and grabbed my hand, pulling me down to my knees so that I was eye to eye with the little guy. "Listen hon. . . I mean Ruby. What I told your mother was the truth and what I said back there is true too. A prophecy is not exact, it can't be. But I swear you are the one that will save the downtrodden from the evil ones, I just know it. Believe me, Ruby, this time I got it right – really I have."

I stood up and brushed the dirt off of my knees and looked at the other two as they stood from their former positions. "This time, dragon? Well is it true that two different races can't have a baby?" I asked the other two in the cave.

The old man and fae stared at each other for a few seconds then looked back at me. The old man shrugged his shoulders as the fae said, "Well to tell you the truth, Ruby Red, none of us have ever gotten along well enough to try if you know what I mean."

"Okay yeah got it. TMI," I said as I looked down at the dragon who was staring up at me with these lost puppy dog eyes. Oh for heaven sakes I thought now that is just pathetic. I looked up at the other two and shook my head. "Well, I guess we go with the dragon's word until we figure out something better unless one of you has another idea?"

No one said a word in the dimly lit tunnel. In the silence I heard the drip of water from somewhere ahead of us. I glanced around and once again that feeling of the space around us closing in asserted itself and a light sweat broke over my whole body. "Are you alright, young lady?"

I heard the old man's voice echo off of the tunnel walls and insert itself into my fears of enclosed places. I jerked myself out of my thoughts and looked at the three that were now giving me an intense stare. "Yeah, yeah fine. I'll just be glad when we get out from here."

The old man nodded at my words as the dragon gave me a sympathetic look. The fae on the other hand shook her head and snorted quietly. Throwing a quick glare her way I asked, "And what's your problem, Tinkerbell."

Shane marched the short distance and got into my personal space so that I had to take a step back from the anger that painted her face. "The problem is, Ruby Red, I doubt very much that you are part fae at all. If I didn't know any better, I would think that between the dragon's stupid prophecy and what that shifter put your mother through that . . ."

I took a step forward so that now I was in the fae's face and snarled, "Listen, you dumb fairy, my mom carried me and she had me and she is my mother and if you . . . you . . ." I stopped as it was getting hard to talk. Then I felt that feeling of itching all over my body and I could feel my claws and canines start to extend.

I felt the old man step to my side and watched through the red veil of anger that clouded my eyes as the fae turned white and took several hasty steps away from me. She whispered, "Damn, is she changing?"

I could hear the dragon shout in happiness as I bent over in pain. "SEE? SEE? I TOLD YOU ALL THAT SHE IS THE ONE!"

The pain of change wasn't as bad today as it had been last night, but I still felt the muscles creak and pull as my wolf asserted herself. As the change finished, I could hear the old man whisper to the fae, "No, stay where you are. A zombie coming after her couldn't induce a change, but her anger with you did. It might be wise if you just stay still until she has full control of herself."

I slowly stood from where I had been crouched and took in the three that crowded the tunnel, focusing on the fae and seeing her through a red haze of anger and once more smelling that underlying sense of fear coming from her. A growl escaped my lips and saliva dripped from my fangs at the thought of sinking my teeth into that soft flesh. I saw with some satisfaction that she reached for the two toys that she carried across her back. She paused with her hands on the hilts but, at the old man's slight head shake, didn't pull her blades.

I took a step forward and then stopped as I watched the pulse at her neck beat to the rhythm of her heartbeat. No, this was a friend. A friend that was a pain but a friend nonetheless; this was not the one that I was after.

I relaxed my body and as I did I could see that the other three followed suit. Even the fae lowered her hands from the sheathed silver blades that crossed her back. She stepped forward and looked at me and then over at the old man. "Well now that we know she can change again, what do we do with her?"

I glanced at the old man as he chuckled, "Put her to sleep, fae. What else?"

"Wait. . ." I started to say when I saw movement out of the corner of my eye and Shane blew something into my face. The next thing I saw was the tunnel floor rushing up to meet me and a darkness that grew suddenly blacker.

OOOOO

Michael had contacted the people he needed after Wilkins informed him of the other crews of shifters that were now invading Bellingham. As he drove to meet the little group he had assembled for tonight's mission, he congratulated himself for being able to land the officer on a police force that was, for the most part, made up of shifters of one sort or another.

Humans, little by little in this small town, were working their way into parts of the government and areas of law enforcement, but it was a slow-going task. They would never be allowed in the top spots, of course, but they were getting people into areas where they could gather what information they could to help the cause. Hell, they even had some Supernaturals that weren't happy with way things were run from Seattle and were leaning towards the human way of thinking about some things.

Michael laughed out loud at the thought of humans and

Supers working together and shook his head in wonderment at the idea. He pulled up to a dark, empty clearing on the outskirts of Bellingham and shut off the car since he had a few minutes before everyone showed up for this little meet. Powering down his window to let a cool night breeze flow through the vehicle, he thought over all the possibilities of where a fae and werewolf would hide. He laughed once more as one name came to mind and the first of his men arrived in the clearing.

Michael hopped out of the car and moved over to the truck carrying the weapons that they would need for this night's work. The driver slowly got out of the truck. Clapping him on the back, Michael asked, "Nice to see you, George, what have you got for me?"

George gave a nervous smile, nodded at the back of the truck and the two of them walked to the end of the covered bed. "I got us some new stuff, Michael, from the military."

Michael looked around the dark clearing and then up at the night sky as though expecting assault troops to drop in on them any second. "What did you get and how did you get it?"

The quiet man's smile lit up the night as he pulled open the door on the back of the truck and yanked out a small wrapped package that was lying inside. "This is what I got for us. And the how? Well, do you really want to know, Michael?" the man said has he handed the package over to his section leader.

Michael thought about it for a few seconds and then shook his head. George was right. As long as he could supply weapons that they could use to fight the Supers there was no reason for him to know where they came from. So far their supply man for his section had never let them down. "No, you're right. I don't need to know the how, just the what."

George nodded at this and then pointed to the package in Michael's hands. "Well, go ahead and take a gander."

Michael unwrapped the weapon like a kid with a new toy at Christmas, tossing the cloth back into the bed of the truck. He looked down at the small shotgun that he held in his hands and noticed that it had four round tubes connected under the barrel. "Okay, it's a shotgun; so I'll bite – what makes it so special?"

George took the weapon from his section leader and showed him a small switch at the side of the weapon and started to give Michael his first lesson. "This particular weapon is a sixteen shot assault weapon. Each barrel here under the main one holds four shells that are combination iron and silver flechette ammo. Basically, instead of buckshot, it shoots little darts."

"Okay that's wicked enough, but how's it work?"

"Easy," George said bringing the weapon up and dry firing four times. You just shoot your ammo load from this barrel, then hit this little switch here with your thumb, rotate the barrel with your other hand and then you have a load of four more shots. With the load you have in this baby, if you practice enough, you can clear a room of Supers in seconds."

Michael looked down at the shotgun and then back up at George. "Well, I must say you do find us the best tools to do the job," he said as he gave another hearty slap to the man's back. "Now the question is you got enough of these things for what we have to do tonight?"

George didn't say a word as he turned back toward the truck and started to pull more wrapped packages from the back. Michael grinned and then looked out over the clearing at the sound of other vehicles arriving for this night's mission. Yeah, he thought, with these little babies in his men's hands they just might have a fighting chance against any Supers that they ran into tonight.

# DINNER TIME

Marcus paced back and forth in the Bellwether Hotel's plush suite, growling and cursing about having to deal with problems in such a backwater town as Bellingham. Most of the crew that were able had fled the scene of their leader's temper tantrum. Experience had taught them that he would lash out at any second at the first crew member that made some tiny error in judgment, most likely an error that would be the unlucky shifter's last.

There was a soft knock on the room door which froze the shifter leader in his tracks and made those that could not leave the room jump a little in nervous anticipation. Marcus stared at the door, his look conveying all the frustration and anger that filtered through the large shifter's system when another knock sounded, this time a little louder than the first. "Well come in, damn it, don't just stand in the hallway waiting for an invitation."

The shifter in charge of communications for this jaunt up the highway from Seattle poked his head around the door and looked in at his leader. "All our crews are here, sir, and ready to tear this pissant place apart to find your daughter."

Marcus looked at the shifter and sneered at the man's fear of stepping into the room to deliver his news and decided that it was time to cut some of this deadwood from his organization. Actually, it was past time to get some shifters in who didn't quake at the first sign of his temper. Yeah, it was time to get shifters that had some balls and would stand up to him.

As this thought drifted through his mind, the men around him looked at the communications expert and knew that playing it safe around Marcus when he was in this mood was the best way to play it. All of them had seen what happened to any shifter that showed the spirit to stand up to their leader. No, what they all knew was that Marcus wanted shifters around him that were tough, but obeyed his every command with no questions asked.

"Anything from the rat yet?" the shifter growled at his communications man.

"No sir."

Marcus glanced out the windows of his room overlooking the night sea lit up from the various boats that were anchored out in the bay. The calm picture that showed outside his window distracted him for a few seconds until his attention was drawn back toward the door when the shifter, still standing halfway in the room, said something that he didn't catch which once more set off his temper.

"What was that you mumbled?"

The man straightened up, throwing a look of defiance at his leader then quickly glanced down at the floor. "I asked what you wanted the crews to do, sir, about finding your daughter and the fae."

Marcus's eyes narrowed at the shifter and the thought crossed his mind that maybe this guy was getting too uppity for his own good, totally forgetting that just seconds ago he was wanting this same man to show some fighting spirit. "Tell the crews that we wait two more hours and if we don't hear from the rat by then we will tear this town down brick by brick and damn what the Shifter Council thinks."

Everyone started at that command and looks were exchanged between the different occupants of the room. Going against Council rules was never done, for that could make an organization outlaw and everyone open game to be killed on sight by any Supernatural.

Marcus glanced around the room, daring anyone to contradict his orders but since no one wanted to die right then not one of the wolf shifters said a word. Marcus looked over at the creature still halfway in the door and growled, "Well? Why are you still standing there? Go tell them what I said. "

As the door shut, Marcus's phone rang stopping the pacing shifter in his tracks once more. He knew that there was only one person that would dare call his private number and cringed at having to listen to her voice again.

All the other shifters seemed to melt into the woodwork, for they all knew who the caller was too and, if Marcus was bad – she was a thousand times worse. With some reluctance, the shifter pushed the answer button on his phone never once contemplating not taking the call.

"Yes dear, what is it now?" he snarled, but the look of annoyance was soon wiped off his face as he listened to the voice on the other end of the phone. A few times the shifter tried to interrupt the strident voice that issued from the phone, but out of habit gave up soon enough.

Finally, after fifteen minutes a cowed Marcus sighed and said, "Yes dear." Hitting the end button, he grumbled in the now quiet room, "I should have killed that woman a long time ago." Then he quickly looked up at the blank faces staring back at him from the room's edges. With a quick glance around, the shifter headed toward his bedroom to brood on his own.

OOOOO

The communications supervisor left the room and slammed the door as he hurried to follow his orders, the whole time thinking that maybe he should let someone in the Council know just what was going on around here. He stopped outside the communications room, thinking. If his notification to the Council was found out, Marcus would have his hide nailed to his office wall. Then he shook his head. If he didn't alert the Council and Marcus went through with his plan, they were all dead anyways.

Hell, even the idea that Marcus was thinking of going against Council rules could get them killed and not in a fast way either. With that decided the shifter knew he had to cover his butt as well as he could and headed into the communications room to give the crews their orders and to make a few calls of his own.

OOOOO

Mack walked the downtown streets of Bellingham with a purpose, avoiding the few shifters he saw knowing that the word was probably out that he be detained and brought back to Marcus's room at the Bellwether Hotel. The rat though had a more important job to do for his new master and Davey was far less forgiving than the wolves were.

The shifter came to the end of the row of downtown buildings and stopped in the parking lot of a Jiffy Lube and looked around in the dark parking lot for any sign of the vamp. Mack was concerned for a few seconds since this was where his master said he would meet him, then the concern changed to fright as he felt an icy cold hand slip around the back of his neck making him jump and actually give out a small squeal.

"What's the matter, dude? I thought shifters were made of braver stuff than that," the soft whisper in the air from the vamp also echoing inside the shifter's head.

The rat stiffened at the implied insult and then his head dropped in shame since the vamp was right. A real shifter would have tried to fight the hold that this creature had over him. Out of the corner of his eye, Mack saw the sly smile of the vamp and the urge to wipe it off of his face died as the vamp tightened his hand on the back of his neck eliciting another squeal from the shifter. This time though the sound was one of pain instead of fright. "Now, now, rat, remember I can see your every thought. So if you don't want me to snap this little neck of yours like a twig I would watch what you are thinking – understand me, shifter?"

"Yes," came back a quiet whisper.

"Yes what, rat?" the vamp's voice rose in the night air as the smile vanished off his face and his eyes once more took on the color of a dead fish.

"Yes, master," came back in an even meeker reply from the rat.

The vamp gave a little chuckle as he slid his hand off the shifter's neck and then gave him a hearty slap on the back. "See, dude? Now that wasn't so hard, was it? Rat, you play by my rules and everything will be just fine. You wait and see. We will be besties in no time."

Mack gave a quick nod of his head, sure that nothing would be fine as long as this monster was around then quickly stifled that thought as the smile once more left the vamp's face. "I found what you were looking for, master," the rat said quickly trying to distract the vamp from whatever thoughts were flowing through his mind right that second.

Davey stared at the shifter for a few seconds then a beaming smile returned to his face. "Good, very good dude, are there a lot of humans in the place?"

"Yes sir, sorry, I thought you could see them through my eyes."

The vamp looked up to the stars above, sighed and mumbled, "Yes most of the time I can, but since I lost so many of my pets at one time, for some reason my power has diminished. I can only see through your eyes and in your mind when we are close like this."

Mack didn't say a word or let a thought flow through his brain that the vamp could pick out, but he filed this new information away for later use, if there was ever going to be a later for a rat that was caught between wolf shifters and a crazy vamp.

Davey came out of the semi-trance he had been in for the few seconds while he was looking up at the night sky and wondered what he had just said to the shifter standing next to him. He had been noticing lately that he had been doing more and more of this kind of thing, where he zoned out and couldn't remember anything about these blank spots. Looking over at the shifter he growled, "Did I just say something to you, rat?"

Trying to keep his mind as blank as he could, Mack shook his head at the vamp and whispered, "No master. You just were standing here looking up at the night sky, sir."

The vamp stared hard at the rat, but nothing disturbing came across his mind so Davey relaxed as the thought of the fun he would have in the next few minutes filtered through his own brain. "Okay then, rat, we are wasting time just standing here. Show me where all these humans are so that I can make some new pets."

"Yes sir," Mack said as he turned and started to walk back down the street toward the noisy bar that was placed in the middle of the block. The two men stopped outside the doors as loud music thumped through the walls and seeped outside.

Davey stood and stared through the windows at the Saturday night crowd that packed the bar and tables. Even more were playing pool at the numerous tables and he gave the rat shifter a quick smile before turning back and looking at the movement inside. "Oh, dude this is perfect, just perfect."

Mack nodded at the compliment and watched as the vamp moved toward the door leading into the bar. "So can I go now, sir?"

The vamp turned, a gleeful smile painting his face as he whispered, "Oh no rat, I need you to stay here and watch the door for about ten minutes. Just hold anyone that comes to the bar outside so that I will have a meal for my new pets when I'm done turning them."

Mack nodded as the vamp slipped through the door where, after a few minutes, the music stopped and not a sound could be heard. The shuffling of feet in the night air followed by the laughter of the four couples that walked down the sidewalk was overly loud in the quiet as they came up to the door of the bar.

"Old man, what's up? There a problem here? They throw you out or something?" a small ratty-faced young man from the group asked amid laughter from the other three men and giggles and twitters from the girls that were with them.

The shifter looked the smaller man up and down, noticing the pants hanging down almost to his knees and the cap that was sitting sideways on his head. The smell of alcohol wafted from the group along with the distinctive smell of something else. "We're closed, go somewhere else if you want to see the morning sunlight."

One of the other men stepped up and looked down at the shifter, a frown crossing his face. "You threatening us, old man?"

The shifter shook his head and, as he was about to speak, the door opened up. Davey stepped out. He pushed past the rat and moved forward so that the bigger man in front of Mack had to take a step back. "Now, now my good man no need for there to be trouble. What my friend here meant was that we were closed for a few minutes because we were at capacity for this establishment, but it seems that we have just enough room for your little group."

The little guy who first spoke up stepped forward and

looked the vamp up and down, frowning at the shifter, "Yeah well that's good, 'cause I'm somebody important in this town and I know the owners of this place, so you had better get this old man out of our way and let us in to party."

The vamp nodded at each word spilling from the small man, a large smile plastered on his face. "Oh why yes, I remember the owner just saying something to me about you coming and that he couldn't wait until you got here. In fact, I think he is just dying to eat—I mean meet you. So why don't you young people just come right on in," Davey said with a little bow and with a flourish he opened the bar door.

One of the young ladies seemed to hesitate until the small mouthy man turned to her and snarled, "Come on, bitch, what's your problem?"

Mack could see the eyes of the vamp change color as he stared at the boy and then turned to the girl, looking deep into her eyes and said, "Perhaps, my dear, you need to go home. You don't look well. You should find someone a little more respectful of your love. Now go before I change my mind."

The young girl got this faraway look on her face, turned and started to walk away from the bar when the small man stepped toward the vamp with a sneer written on his face. "Hey, no one tells my bitch what to do, I . . ."

The vamp gave each of the remaining group that same

captivating look and they all got that same faraway look in their eyes. "Never mind her, we are going to have so much fun in here, especially you and me my small young friend," the vamp said as he draped his arm over the small man's shoulder and pulled him inside.

As the group filed past him, Mack could hear the vamp inside his head give him a little pat and directions to watch the door for any more meals on wheels that happened to walk by. The door shut on the group and a few seconds later Mack listened as the music started up again, but even over the thumping of the band, he could hear the screams of the group as the newly made zombies descended upon their meal. The shifter turned to look at the door as he heard a wet slap and saw the little rat-faced man trying to get it open. Then a dozen zombies grabbed him from behind and pulled him into the crowd, ripping and tearing flesh and soon all he could hear was the sound of music once more coming from the bar. As he turned back to the street, two more couples came staggering up the sidewalk and the shifter held open the door to their death.

OOOOO

I slowly opened my eyes to the dim light in the tunnel and felt a slight pounding in my head as I sat up and looked around. The first thing I saw was the fae sitting on a rock with her back to me and the thought of quietly moving up behind her and smacking her over the head for what she had done to me crossed my still addled mind.

"Since you're up now how about you throw those clothes on so we can catch up to the cat and the dragon," Shane whispered, her back still toward the dark opening of the cave.

That's when I noticed that once again the clothes I had been wearing were in tatters and lying all around me. I could see that this whole werewolf thing was going to be hell on the clothing budget. I glanced around and saw a small pile of things and quickly threw them on without acknowledging the presence of the fae who sat in the same spot she had when I woke up.

When I finished throwing on the shirt and pants that were there, I noticed that my shoes had survived my latest change and sat down on a rock across from the fae to get them on my feet. After that quick little chore was done, I got up without a word and started to walk down the tunnel when her words stopped me. "You know, Ruby Red, you do wake up pretty crabby after your change. It must be the shifter side of you."

I turned, looking to blast the little fae with some choice words when I noticed this huge smile plastered across her face and she said, "Made you look." I gave a grunt of annoyance, grabbed the flashlight and started back up the tunnel as I heard her hop off the rock and her small feet move to catch up to me.

We walked in silence for quite awhile before the fae grabbed my arm and stopped me in my tracks. With some surprising strength, she turned me to face her and gave a little laugh as I looked over her head at the black tunnel behind us. "Oh, real mature there, Ruby Red. Are you going to ignore me the whole time we are in this tunnel?"

Yeah, Shane was right, I probably was acting like a two-year-old that had had her favorite toy taken away, but right now I wasn't feeling in control of my life and it was really affecting my thinking. I looked down at the fae and shook my head at her as a few tears ran down my cheeks. "I thought you were my friend."

Shane stood there, a look of shock on her face wiping out the smile as it all came flooding out of me. "I mean you helped me before with the werewolves and then to escape, but since then you act like you barely care. You make me go through the change and then put me to sleep, and . . ."

The fae's grip on my arm tightened and I dropped the flashlight I was holding as a small frown spilled across her face. "I'm sorry, Ruby Red, that I gave you that impression that we are friends. I promised your mother that I would help train you. I made that promise because she once tried to save someone that was very close to me. You are a shifter, one of my sworn enemies and if the Queen, your Grandmother, knew exactly what you were she would most likely have you killed."

"Oh, so we aren't friends?" I asked meekly.

Shane looked down at the ground and then back up at me – her face a blank slate. "I don't make friends, Ruby Red, for in this world friends die. So no, we are not friends."

I glanced around, feeling stupid for thinking that the fae was more than someone just doing her job. "Oh, well I see then. Well, I won't trouble you anymore then." With that, I started down the tunnel but stopped as the dark descended on me.

Behind me, I could hear the fae give a small chuckle and saw from the shadows that were now bouncing off the walls that she had picked up the flashlight and was walking down the tunnel toward me. "Want a little light to walk by, Ruby Red?"

Since the fae had made it clear that she wasn't my friend and had no interest in me other than my training, I once more ignored her and stood there waiting until she caught up to me. Shane shrugged her shoulders and sighed then started walking down the tunnel with me following behind her. The silence of the tunnel was only interrupted by the footfalls that echoed off the walls.

OOOOO

We walked for quite awhile without a word exchanged between the two of us when we came to the end of the tunnel. Like the other end, I could see a white line painted on the ground and spied the small box that probably held the detonator switches that would take down this end of the tunnel and whatever building was beyond these dark walls.

When we got to the end of the tunnel, the fae stopped and started to feel around the wall as she told me, "The dragon and the old man went ahead while you slept to make sure that his other home was clear. Since they didn't come back, I assumed that everything is okay. There we go." With a click, the wall slid forward and we stepped into a cave that was an exact duplicate of the one we had left behind.

I looked at the old man and the dragon sitting in some chairs and wondering what was wrong with the picture in front of me when I heard a low voice from my right say, "Anyone moves or even twitches just a little, me and my boys here will send you to the other side."

That's when I noticed that the old man and the dragon were sitting tied to their chairs and had tape across their mouths. I started to set myself to spring toward the voice when I heard the fae's whisper, "Don't Ruby Red, there is too many of them."

I eased back down to the flat of my feet as I noticed that as usual Shane was right as more men stepped out of the black shadows of the cave. I looked closer at the weapon that each man carried and gave a little gulp as I realized that I would have never stood a chance against the ammo that those things could probably throw in the air.

That's when I felt a small buzz in the air and all that were standing in the room were frozen. I looked around at all of them, humans, fae, shifters, and the dragon. Not one of them moved nor even blinked and then I was startled by the sweet mellow voice that sounded right behind my ear.

# THE ONE

Marcus was still stalking the hotel room. The two-hour time limit he had set passed. One of the braver enforcers gave a small cough and watched with some fear in his eyes as their leader stopped in the middle of the room and gave a little growl then bit it back with a deep sigh. This whole business was driving the wolf in him to distraction. The thought crossed his mind that after almost nineteen years of waiting, he really needed to finish this business with his daughter tonight.

Silence dominated the room with everyone lost in their own thoughts until the phone rang, sounding overly loud in the enforced quiet. The closest enforcer answered the call and stood there listening to the whispered voice on the other side. The voice was so low that even the other wolves in the room couldn't hear the words spoken despite their excellent hearing.

"For you, sir," the enforcer said holding the phone out to his leader. "It's the rat."

Marcus stood there for a few seconds and then slowly walked over to the nightstand and took the phone out of the shifter's hand. "You're late, rat. What took you so long?"

"Sorry sir, but I did what you wanted me to," the rat said. Something in Mack's voice once again triggered a small warning in the back of the wolf's mind. It wasn't so much what the rat had said as how he was saying it that pinged at his subconscious. Marcus had dealt with this particular creature for a long time and he knew, even over the phone, that the rat had lost what fear of him he had built up over the years.

Marcus hesitated for just a second then shook his head as to wash away the feeling that was bothering him. "I think, rat, when we see each other again we need to teach you the meaning of respect to your betters."

There was quiet on the other end of the line then the rat's voice once more sounded through the phone, this time a certain note of subservience coming through the line and wiping the last reservations of unease from the wolf shifter's mind. "I'm sorry, sir. I didn't mean to cause trouble, sir. Please forgive me. I just meant that I now have the information that you need to find the vamp, along with the fae and your daughter."

A large smile crossed the wolf's face at the proper groveling and sniveling the rat seemed to be exhibiting to his superior. Yes, this was a much better attitude that the rat was showing. Who knows, maybe after all this was over and if the creature's information was valuable he might just keep him alive. "Much better attitude, rat," he growled pacified that all was back to the way it should be. "Now where can I find the ones that I want, rat?"

"Well, sir, you are in luck for all the ones you want will be in one place tonight."

There was a pause and Marcus was once more feeling that unease seep into his bones for this was all too easy to have all his prey in one spot. "I don't want to ask again, rat. If I do you won't live through the night."

There was a small chuckle on the other end of the line so low that even the wolf wasn't sure that he had heard right. "Yes, sir, no worries. The vamp will be at that old cat's house. You know the one that helps the young ones go through their change in this area."

Marcus's temper flared at the thought of that damn cat in league with a vamp. It figured, he thought, you could never trust those felines, loners as they were thinking that they were better than all other shifters. Well, this is one cat that was going to learn just who was the boss in this territory. The wolf's mind was occupied with these thoughts and he missed the rat's next words and had to stop him in mid-sentence to catch up with what the shifter was saying. "What? What was that, rat?"

"Sorry, sir, I said that the vamp will be at the old cat's house because that is where your daughter and the fae are.

Seems that he helped your daughter in her first change and then they ran into some little problems with the vamp's zombies."

Panic clutched at the wolf's heart for a second at the thought of zombies that the vamps used in all their dirty work, but he managed to push that feeling down at the rat's next words. "It seems that the cat destroyed the vamp's pets at his old house somehow and made his way to his second home across the mountains."

The thought of the vamp all on his own brought a smile to the wolf's face and all those that were close enough to hear the voice over the phone. For no matter how powerful the shifters were, zombies in any size group could tear through a shifter pack with ease. "So are you sure that the vamp is all on his own then?"

"Oh yes, sir, quite all on his lonesome. Now if you want, I can email the directions to you on how to get to the old cat's house."

"What? Yes, fine, rat, do that and I want you to meet us there. You got me, rat? I want to give you a big reward for all this great information you have given me."

Mack knew exactly what kind of reward he would get from the wolves, but played along hoping that his new master would keep him in one piece in the fight to come. He emailed the directions that the vamp had given him wondering if the others were really at this place or if it was just a set up to get the wolves somewhere where the zombies could have a free shot at them. "Oh yes sir, I can't wait to get my reward from you, sir. I will be there waiting for you in one hour, sir."

Marcus looked at the email that he had just opened from the rat, on his own phone, and saw just how far out in the boonies that the old cat's house was. "Yeah well you do that rat, but it will take us a little longer than that to get up there in those mountains. Maybe like two hours for us to get there. So just make sure that you are not seen by the vamp or the others before we get there or you will be on your own. Understand me, rat?"

"Oh, of course, sir . . ." Mack started to answer, but he was talking to a dead phone line. The shifter clicked off his phone and slipped it into his pocket as he walked over to the vamp who stood in the middle of the clearing. "They are on their way, master, now if I could just leave . . ."

The vamp tore his eyes away from the stars that he was gazing at and smiled at his toy. "No, I don't think so just yet, dude. I think that if the wolves show up at our little meeting place and don't see you they will be a little suspicious. Besides, didn't that dog say that he has a big reward for you, rat? You wouldn't want to miss out on that now, would you?" the vamp said his eyes turning a light shade of white and his fangs extending slightly below his upper lip.

Mack took a step back and bowed to the vamp. "Yes, of course, you are totally right, master."

"Yes I am, aren't I, bro? Now let us go get my pets for I think they are hungry for a little dog chow," the vamp said with a laugh as he turned and walked off into the night with the rat following obediently behind him.

OOOOO

Marcus slammed the phone down in the middle of the rat's conversation and turned to look at all the shifters in the room. "This is where we are going," he said as he tossed his phone over to one of his enforcers. "Get all our people together and get ready to move out in fifteen minutes."

The shifter enforcer looked at the directions then stopped and turned to Marcus with some confusion written on his face. "Sir, it shouldn't take us two hours to get to this place, I . . ."

Marcus shook his head wondering at the brainless wits that he was surrounded by then growled, "Of course it won't take us that long you idiot, but the rat doesn't know that now shut up and get all the men together. We leave in thirteen minutes now."

The enforcer cringed and then hurried out the door of the room to do his leader's bidding. Marcus watched as he closed the door and then turned to the other shifters in the room. "He doesn't come back with us. Got me?" They all gave a nasty smile to their leader, but inside all of them were wondering when that same order would be given about them.

OOOOO

"Hello dear." It was a soft whisper just behind my left ear.
I started in the sudden quiet and turned to see – nothing.
There wasn't anyone else in the room besides those of us
who had been there before the sudden freezing of all the
bodies.

God, I thought, I had finally gone and done it. I had lost
what little mind that I had left tonight. The voice sounded
from behind me again, "No, dear, you have not lost your
mind. I was in the area and decided to have a little girl-to-
girl talk with you, shall we say?"

I slowly turned and then closed my eyes to tiny slits as a
bright light blinded me and once more I heard the sweet
voice say, "Oh, sorry my dear. Here, how is this?" With her
words the light dimmed to a small glow and before me
stood a little girl who had to be at least ten years younger
than I was from all appearances.

"That's better, I guess. Thanks?" I said as I opened my eyes
wide and took in the beauty that stood before me. She was
no taller than four feet and I could probably have put both
my hands around her waist, she was so skinny. Her hair
was the color of wheat in the sunlight and it flowed around
her head as though it had a life of its own. Her skin was
this flawless milk-white color with just the hint of rose at
her cheeks.

I felt like I had been entranced by her for what seemed like
forever when that sweet voice sounded once more. "Cat

got your tongue, my dear?" she said with what I swear was a slight girlish giggle.

I shook my head as though coming out of a trance and looked around at all those still frozen around me. "Sorry kid, but just who are you? And what have you done to everyone?"

The little girl smiled at me and then looked at the others around the room. "Well as for the second part of your question, I haven't done anything that will hurt these poor creatures in this room, so you can stop worrying about that part. As for the first part of your question, I am the One."

"Okay, the one what, exactly?"

The little girl gave a small silver laugh that tinkled in the air like small bells. "The One, my dear. You know the One that created all things, the stars, the worlds, all the peoples in all the cosmos. That One, my dear," she said pointed up toward the heavens with those tiny little fingers.

I looked at the small being in front of me and my legs gave out. I started to fall to the floor but was stopped when my butt parked itself in a chair that was suddenly behind me. Oh and here I thought I was losing it before now someone just needs to come and wrap me up in a straightjacket, take me to the rubber room and throw away the key. "Sorry kid, but really I have had a long couple of days and I really don't think I can take anymore . . ."

The next thing I knew, I was standing in front of the small

girl surrounded by stars and planets. I looked as they twirled around us and then looked on as she held up a small spinning ball that I recognized as my own world. "I am the One, my dear, the creator of all life on this world and millions more." Then once more we were inside the cave.

I don't know if I felt faint at the rush of being wherever we had been and then back here or what, but I felt myself start to go black when I heard that small silver laugh once more. "Oh, my dear I thought you were made of stronger stuff than that. Now come on, dear, buck up and sit up for we need to talk, just us two girls."

I shook my head back and forth at the voice, a small whisper escaping my lips. "Oh, this is so not happening. I mean aren't you supposed to be this old man with a long beard and . . . oh, my . . ."

That's when I felt her soft hand gently touch my arm and my head cleared. I looked up into eyes of dark blue. Looking deeper into them, I could see the same stars that we had just been standing in swirl and spin in their depths. "Oh my, you are the One."

That smile came again, washing away the look of concern on her face and filling me with hope and strength. "Why yes, of course, I am my dear. I would never lie to one of my children."

"Oh, well no problem, I mean I didn't think you were lying to me per se as that, like I said before, I have had a rough couple of nights and days as it is."

The young girl just nodded at me as I spoke, the look of concern riding once more across her face. "I know, my dear, and that is why I am here right now. To explain as well as I can what you need to do, well what you and your sister need to do that is."

"I think you may have the wrong person, not to be disrespectful or anything, but I don't have a sister."

It was surprising how she could just stand there and look at you as you talked and you felt that your words were the only sound she heard. She nodded at my words then glanced over to where the dragon was sitting on his seat still frozen as the others were. "I see someone forgot to mention that little fact, my dear." She once more focused on me and that smile lit up her face again. "Why, of course, you have a sister. A little sister, in fact. And once you are done here in this land, you and my watcher will go and get your sister so that you two can fulfill your destiny. Isn't that right, Percy?"

The dragon started and then slid off the chair and bowed before the young girl. Where all the rope and tape that had bound him only seconds ago went, I didn't ponder. "Oh yes, my mistress, it is as you say."

The young girl stood there shaking her head at the dragon and admonished him. "Percy, how many times have I told you not to do that and why are you still taking that silly dragon form?"

The dragon stood up quickly and looked around at his body and then up at the girl before him. "Why, Mistress, I like this form and besides I think it suits me, don't you?"

This was said with a small look of concern that melted the heart of the little girl and she reached out and gave him a quick hug while chuckling, "Why, of course, you are right, Percy. You look absolutely perfect in that form."

I looked between those two at this exchange and closed my eyes and shook my head at the sight. At the quiet laughter that floated through the air, I once more opened my eyes and saw that both the small girl and the dragon were looking at me with smiles written on both their faces. "So, you know each other then?"

"Oh why, of course, I know Percy, my dear. He is the one who is responsible for keeping an eye on this world for me."

"Oh, so you're just so busy that you can't keep an eye on the people in this world? I thought that if you were the One that you would be all powerful and all seeing and all that garbage."

After I was done with this little rant, I thought for sure that I would see some sign of anger in the girl's face, but once more all I caught was that look of concern. "Oh my dear I am so sorry, but you see when I created all the worlds and all the stars, well basically all of creation I had so many creatures to look after on all the different worlds that I made watchers that would help me look after them all."

I took in all she said and then glanced at Percy and then back at the girl. "You mean there are others out there, like us?"

The girl shook her head at my surprise and gave a little laugh. "Why, of course, there are others out there, my dear. What did you think – that with all the stars and worlds out there that you were the only creatures that I made? This creation of mine is so vast that your mind could not comprehend how wide and huge it really is and for that reason, I have assigned a watcher for each world." She quickly glanced at Percy and then back at me. "Of course, some watchers may be a little better than others."

I couldn't help but give a little snicker as Percy's face fell and he gave a little snort of indignation, but the snicker died at the young girl's next words and the thoughtful look on her face. "Of course I could just start over on this world."

I jumped up from the chair as Percy grabbed hold of the young girl's arm and gave her a pleading look. I wasn't one hundred percent sure what she meant by starting over on this world, but I had a pretty good idea it wouldn't be good for those of us that live here.

The girl looked down at Percy and smiled. "I don't know, what do you think about cockroaches, Percy? I mean as creatures they really don't cause much harm, or say . . ."

"Oh no mistress I think that you need to give Ruby here and her sister a chance, don't you? I mean after all I did give out a prophecy and it would be very bad manners not to see it through."

The girl glanced over at the dragon and then looked up at me once more that smile brightening the cave and all that stood in it. "Well, I guess you are right. I should give them a chance, but I warn you, Percy, the next time that I come here this world had better be cleaned up and the creatures not running around killing each other. I swear I have none of this kind of trouble on any of my other worlds. I just don't see why this one is such a bother."

Percy let go of the girl's arm, whipped off his hat and gave such a low bow that I thought I saw his nose scrape the ground. "Oh thank you, mistress you are as forgiving as you are beautiful . . ."

"Enough with the bull Percy it's getting pretty deep around here with the way you're flinging it around. I said I would give these girls a chance, just so it doesn't turn out as bad as that vamp idea of yours, you hear me, dragon, or that whole fiasco with the dinosaurs."

The young girl gave the dragon one more glance and then turned to me. "Alright, my dear, you have one year to straighten out this crazy world, so good luck and ta-ta. I have other worlds to visit." And with that, she was gone.

I looked around expecting the others in the cave to be unfrozen with the girl's departure, but everyone still stood or sat in the case of the old man in the exact spot they had been before. "Percy, I think she forgot something."

The dragon stood there looking at the floor for a few seconds then started as I called his name once more. "What? What was that, Ruby?"

I looked at the dragon and then around at all the people still frozen. "I said I think she forgot something. The little girl, when she left, she forgot to unfreeze everyone."

The dragon gave a quick look around and then smiled at me. "Oh no, she didn't forget, Ruby. I am keeping them this way for a few minutes while . . ."

"Wow, you can do that? Cool."

The dragon's smile got larger and then he gave a little shake of his head. "Well, I can't do it on my own, but since my mistress was here she left a little residue of magic in the air that I can pull down and use. I just wanted a few seconds alone with you to make sure that you understand that she was very serious about you and your sister changing this world."

I gave a quick shrug and sat down in the chair behind me. "So when she said about starting over on this world she really meant . . ."

Percy gave a couple quick nods of his head and looked over at the wall where a large bug was crawling up it and gave a large shudder. "Yes, she meant exactly that. And if you don't mind, I would rather not be a watcher on a world of cockroaches or maybe slugs. Man she does like her insects, you should see some of the other worlds," he said with another shudder.

"Okay, yeah I could see where that would be creepy, but what was she saying about that thing with the vamps just before she left?"

The dragon got this guilty look on his face if ever there was one and tried to change the subject on me. As he stuttered and stammered, I wouldn't have anything to do with it and finally he spilled the beans. "Oh alright if you must know Ruby, the whole idea for the vamps was mine and it sort of, kind of, maybe didn't work out quite the way I thought it would."

I looked at the dragon and shook my head and gave a little laugh at the look of embarrassment now on his face. "You think it 'kind of' didn't work out, Percy? I mean come on how you even imagined that a creature that turned humans into zombies, not to mention what it does to all the other creatures in this world, would be a good idea."

"Well, when you put it that way Ruby it does sound like a bad idea, but really I had good intentions at the start, and . . ." I never heard what the dragon had to say about his good intentions because right about then all hell broke loose as everyone in the cave became unfrozen at once.

# THE SETUP

Davey looked around the clearing once more as the moonlight shone down through the trees and then turned to the rat shifter next to him. "Nice job I did with my pets don't you think, dude? I mean it takes real finesse and power to bury my pets alive without leaving any trace, don't you think?"

Mack glanced at the vamp and then back at the clearing that surrounded the small cabin that was built into the side of the mountain. The picture that it presented hid the horror that lay just below the ground and he gave a little shudder at the thought of the zombies that were lying just below the surface of the ground. "Yes sir, a really great job, none of the wolves will be able to tell that there is a zombie anywhere around here, but if I may . . ."

Davey looked from the clearing where he was still admiring his recent work and over at the shifter with a small touch of annoyance. "Yes? Yes, what is it, rat?"

"Well, sir can your zombies be able to get out of the ground fast enough to do any real damage to the wolves once they get here?"

The vamp gave a dark little laugh that sent a shiver up and down the rat's spine. "Oh don't worry about that part, bro. My pets are buried just below the surface of the ground and will have no trouble getting out of their resting places to accomplish their work. True, I may lose one or two of them, but that is why I made so many extra, and after all they are just zombies."

Mack thought back to how the vamp had stood over each of his 'pets' as they lay on the ground and as he mumbled words each zombie would slowly melt into the ground as though the solid rock beneath them had suddenly changed to quicksand. He gave one more shudder as the thought of all those semi-dead bodies laying there, just waiting for the command of the vamp next to him to bring them once more to the surface of this world.

Davey was now staring at the cabin across the clearing and started whispering so low that even with his keen hearing Mack had trouble making out the vamp's words. "Now we just need to wait for the wolves to come here and I will be able to protect my love from her father and she will be so grateful that she will fall hopelessly in love with me, dude."

Without thinking the rat shifter turned to the vamp and gave a small laugh and blurted out, "You're kidding, right?"

The vamp moved so fast that the shifter didn't even have

time to realize what was happening to him until he felt his body slammed up against the truck of the tree behind him. He took in what he could of a gulp of air as he looked down into the eyes of death itself. Slowly the fingers that were wrapped around his throat tightened and even the little bit of air that was seeping through was cut off. As he started to black out from the lack of oxygen, he heard the vamp whisper, "I never kid about my love, dude." Then he felt his body fly through the air once more where it impacted another tree, deeper in the woods.

Mack felt himself hanging in the air up against the tree his toes just barely touching the ground. As he looked down and saw a large branch sticking out of the center of his chest, the pain from the impact and the impalement roared through his body. The only sound he could muster was a low groan that was drowned out by the dark laughter of the vamp who was suddenly standing just in front of him. "Damn, bro, that does look pretty painful, bet that must really, really hurt," the vamp said as he reached up and wiggled the end of the tree branch that Mack hung from.

This brought another low moan of pain, the only sound that the rat could muster from the intense feelings that racked his body. "Guess we should get you down from there, don't you think, dude? Boy I really think this is going to hurt you more than it hurts me," the vamp said gleefully as he walked out of the shifter's sight. All Mack could manage was to shake his head in the negative knowing that no matter how the vamp did it taking him down from where he hung would be a thousand times more painful than what he felt right now.

With a loud crack, the shifter felt his feet touch the ground as the vamp broke the branch off of the tree. What air Mack could suck into his destroyed lungs left him as he felt the kick in the back that dislodged him from the branch and sent him flying to the ground.

With a soft groan, he managed to turn over so that he was looking up into the star-filled night sky that was until the vamp's face filled his view. "So was I right, dude? I mean that did look like it really hurt." Mack's glazed eyes looked up at the vamp and all he could muster was a low whimper while he lay there, just hoping that he would die soon so that the pain would stop.

Davey looked down at the shifter with a gleeful smile as he shook his head. "Oh dude, don't worry I'm not going to let you die that easy – remember we're besties, right? Besides, I still need you. Now this is going to hurt like the dickens, rat, and since your friends will be here soon we need to keep quiet." With that the vamp grasped the shifter's mouth with one hand and clamped his jaw shut while with the other he reached down into the chest wound and started to pour raw energy into it.

Mack's body arched up off the ground as though a thousand volts of electricity was flowing through it. The vamp slowly brought his hand out of the wound as the flesh healed under his touch; he poured more and more of his energy into the rat shifter's torn body. Fortunately for the shifter, he passed out from the pain three seconds into the healing.

OOOOO

As everyone became unfrozen, I could see all eyes turn to the dragon and me in confusion since we had moved from the spots that we had been in when all this had started. I caught Shane's movement as she pulled her two swords from behind her and made to leap into the middle of the group of humans while at the same time I heard the distinctive click of safeties being released on the various weapons around us.

If I didn't do something quickly there was going to be a lot of bloodshed around the small cave and I figured that some of it would belong to me. I jumped forward between the two sides holding out both of my arms as though to hold back the tide of violence that was about to erupt around me. "Whoa, whoa, everybody just calm down, we are all on the same side here."

The fae stopped where she stood as the older of the humans paused for a second giving me a searching look then without a word he held up his closed fist. All the humans around the cave stopped moving toward the fae and me but still covered us alertly with their weapons.

The human that seemed in charge stepped up in front of me, giving the fae and the dragon a wary look. I took in his lean frame with the neatly trimmed beard that, along with the short hair he wore, had a sprinkling of gray through it. "And why should we believe that we are on the same side there, young lady?"

I looked him up and down and gave him my best smile. "Let's just say that I got it from a much higher authority that I am supposed to work with the good guys and help the downtrodden."

I don't know from whom, but I heard several snorts of laughter that died as the man before me glanced around at those with him. Then he turned back to me with a small chuckle. "And how do you know we are the good guys, young lady?"

I looked around at the group surrounding us and figured that was a good question. I seemed to be putting my faith in a group that, for all intents and purposes, looked like they would like nothing better to do than to kill the Supers that were in this cave. "Well, first off my name is Ruby, Ruby Red. And second is that if you weren't the good guys then I figured you wouldn't have taken the time to listen to me."

The man gave me an intense stare for a few seconds then seemed to relax a little. "Okay, you got me there young . . . I mean Ruby. Say we are the good guys, what do think that a little slip of a girl like you is going to do against all the things that go bump in the night in this world."

Percy stepped forward and in front of me, getting up close to the man standing there. "She is the savior for all of us.

She is the prophecy, the one that will help all the downtrodden in this world."

The man looked down at the dragon and burst out laughing. The laughter was echoed by the rest of the humans. "Hear that, men? This little girl is going to do what we can't. She is here to save the human race," the man stopped laughing and looked down at Percy with a sneer over his face. "Dragon, I have heard about you and your prophecies. I think maybe me and the rest of the human race will just stick to our weapons if you don't mind."

I dropped my hand on the downcast dragon's shoulder, feeling sorry for the little guy. Granted from all I had heard, he wasn't perfect, well yeah I guess you could say he did have a tendency to screw things up thinking about the vamp and zombies that were out there somewhere, but at least he was trying to help. That's when the fae stepped up next to my side while she put her swords away. "You humans are not the only ones that need help in this world. There are people in all the races that are treated poorly by the select few in charge."

The man just nodded his head at the fae's words while I could see him thinking about the point that she had brought up. "Okay, you have me there. You're right that humans aren't the only ones that suffer at the hands of the few Supers in charge, but we are the ones that take the brunt of the abuse. But that aside, I still don't see how one little girl is going to help anyone get out from under the yoke of the Supers in charge."

Now that we had seemed to have gotten the attention of the human's leader once more, Percy seemed to perk up and put in his two cents worth. "Listen! Ruby here and her sister have the powers of all the Supers inside them. All we need to do is show her how to use that power and then she can fight and win."

"All by herself?" the man said giving me a once over. "That little thing?"

I started to get a little pissed at this attitude. Granted I was small and compact but hadn't I already killed a werewolf and a zombie all on my own. "Fine, so I'm small, so I'm a girl, but I can still fight. Besides who said that I have to do it all on my own, I mean together all of us could take the fight to the Supers who rule and kick their magical butts. I mean from the sound of it there are a whole lot fewer of them than there are of us, right?"

Once more the man glanced around the cave at his men and then back at me. "Yeah you got me there, Ruby, there are a lot more of the downtrodden in the world than the ruling class, but there always is, that's the way of the world we live in. The problem is getting everyone together to make a difference."

I nodded at these words as I saw most of the humans and the fae next to me do. "Well, then I guess that is what we do then. We get together the people that are willing to stand up and fight and then we go out and take over the world."

The man gave me a quick smile. "Well, I must say one thing for you, Ruby, you do have spirit if nothing else you do have that. Okay, so what do we do next?"

With that, the tension in the room seemed to lessen as the men around us lowered their weapons. Then I heard the voice of the old man, still tied in the same chair he had been in when the fae and I came into the cave, speak up, "Well if someone would untie me, I think we should go into my house and make some coffee, where we can talk this over in a more comfortable situation."

One of the humans looked over at the leader as he pulled out a wicked little knife and at the slight nod of his head, cut the ropes and then stepped back as the old man stood up rubbing his wrists as though to get the blood flowing back into his hands. "Thanks much."

The leader of the humans just nodded back and then turned to head toward the other door that I assumed led out of the cave when he turned back to me and held out his hand. "By the way, my name is Michael."

"Nice to meet you, Michael," I said as I shook his hand and we all went out the front door of the cave and into the old man's house.

OOOOO

Marcus looked at his watch as his truck entered the clearing where all his men waited for their leader. He got out of the truck cursing once more the need to be out in the boonies to take care of this problem but promised himself that this would all end tonight. Finally, he would have the daughter that was rightly his at his side and he would use what power she had, if the rumors that were going around were true, to make himself the most powerful Super this side of the ocean.

Climbing out of his SUV, one of his enforcers walked out of the dark and grinned at his leader. "Perimeter is set, sir, no sign of zombie anywhere."

Marcus turned a cold stare at the enforcer that wiped the smile off his face. "What about the old cat's house? My daughter and the fae?"

The enforcer nodded and pointed up the side of the mountain. "The cat's house is straight up there about ten miles. The road gets rough here and I figured we will need to go up on foot to surprise them. I sent three scouts up about ten minutes ago to check our route out. As soon as they recon the cat's house, I figure we could get up there in an hour or so after that, sir."

Marcus nodded; at least this shifter seemed to know his job and was efficient at it. I'll need to keep an eye on this one, he thought, as the fear of some young smarter more ruthless shifter coming up and taking his position once more reared its ugly head in his mind. "Fine, fine keep me posted on what the scouts find." With that Marcus waved the enforcer away and turning walked to the back of the truck that he had ridden up in.

As he walked back, one of his bodyguards opened the back door of the SUV and Marcus smiled down at the small tied up figure that was looking back at him with wide fearful eyes. The shifter looked at the dirty, smelly figure that his men had grabbed out of some back alley and his face lit up even more at the smell of all that delicious fear that came off in waves from the now struggling figure.

Reaching into the back of the truck, the wolf grabbed the struggling girl and headed toward a small patch of dark trees while tossing directions over his shoulders at his bodyguards. "Make sure I'm not disturbed while I'm at dinner unless it is really important."

The chorus of "Yes sirs," drowned out the muffled screams from the small body that heard the horrible fate that awaited her as she was carried into the dark like any common take out meal.

# BATTLE PLANS

The vamp leaned over the prone body of the shifter, giving him a few 'light' taps across the face to bring him back to consciousness. Mack slowly opened his eyes hoping that he was finally dead and out of this whole mess, but the smiling face inches from his dashed that brief hope to dust. "Why hello, dude, welcome back to the living such as it is."

"Should have just let me die, vamp," the shifter moaned out in a low groan as his body shuddered with a small remnant of the pain from the 'healing' that he had gone through.

The vamp gave Mack that crazy smile of his that said that the elevator didn't go all the way to the top as he helped the shifter to sit up. "Now bro, I think you and I are becoming the best of friends. Well, of course, until you piss me off, but hey come on all friends have those little moments, don't they?"

"Yeah, sure whatever you say, Davey. Friends forever,

buddies for life," the shifter moaned figuring that since he was alive for the moment it wouldn't hurt to get on the good side of the vamp again.

The vamp got the shifter to his feet and leaned him against the tree that only seconds ago he had been impaled on. Or had it been longer than that the shifter thought as he looked up at the night sky trying to figure out how long he had been unconscious after the vamp healing powers had hit him. He could still feel the burn of those powers deep within his body as it felt like maybe the vamp hadn't quite gotten everything back exactly where it should have been.

Davey stood there alternating watching the shifter that he was helping to stand on his own two feet and looking down the side of the mountain. Mack heard the tiniest murmur of sound and started to say something when he felt the vamp's hand clamp once more across his mouth as he leaned toward the shifter's ear and whispered, "Looks like some of your other friends have come to play. Now you stay right here for I need to go and get some food since I'm soooo hungry from having to heal you."

With that the vamp was gone in a flash and without his help holding the shifter up, Mack's legs did the sensible thing – they gave out. The shifter slowly slid down the rough bark of the tree until he was sitting once more on the ground. The rat shifter stared off into the dark foliage looking to see if he could tell where the vamp had disappeared to, but the night was as dark and silent as an open grave.

OOOOO

Jordan moved up the side of the mountain cursing his luck in getting picked for this job. Granted he and his fellow teammates were scouts for the organization, being lean, fast, and quiet on their feet even more so than most wolf shifters, but going out on a scout mission in Seattle after some derelict was one thing. Going out into the deep woods on a scout mission for a vamp was a complete suicide mission in his opinion. But of course when you're told by Marcus to do a job it was suicide not to obey so here he and two of his men were out in the night looking for some vamp, the leader's daughter, and a fae no less.

The wolf shifter stopped, thinking that he had heard some movement over to his right, about fifty feet, where one of his teammates should be. He watched the area for a few seconds then reached up and pushed the small button that activated his com unit. "Jones, Jones have you seen anything?" he whispered.

Nothing but dead silence, he was just going to call over to the shifter on his left when he heard the barest whisper of sound in that direction. He momentary looked over in that direction but turned to his front when he felt a presence there. His eyes widened in shock at the sight of the Southern California surfer boy that was standing in front of him. A vamp he had expected, but this image was just so out of place in these woods. It took him a second to register that he couldn't draw any air into his lungs now since the boy before him had one hand clamped around his throat and was squeezing it while bringing his neck closer to the pair of razor sharp fangs that had just extended from his boyish mouth.

OOOOO

In seconds, the wolf shifter that hung from the vamp's hand was drained of all energy. A fate he shared with the other two scouts. Davey noiselessly dropped the darkened shrunken body to the ground and surveyed the surrounding area for any more creatures that he could feed on.

Hearing the static from the com unit that the wolf had been wearing, the vamp took the earpiece off of the dried out body and listened to the voice on the other end. "Jordan, repeat that last message. Jones, are you there? Jordan, answer me . . ."

The vamp, with a smile, adjusted the mouthpiece and pushed the small button that cut off the voice. "Sorry, the party you are trying to contact is not available right now. Please try again later," Davey cackled crazily. With that, the vamp pulled the earpiece out and dropped it next to the drained shifter's body.

The enforcer at the other end stared in horror at the now dead radio then, shaking himself out of his stupor, called out to his team leader.

OOOOO

The two enforcers moved over to the black SUV that the leader was resting in after having his evening meal and knocked on the door. The window rolled down and the dark sinister eyes of Marcus looked out into the night. "What is it?"

"I think the vamp got our scouts, sir . . ."

Marcus popped open the door of the truck and leaped out, taking the team leader with him so that the creature was slammed up against one of the trees that surrounded the clearing. The shifter's nostrils flared in fear and the breeze brought the smell of fresh blood to his nose from the tree line where the remnants of his leader's meal lay. "What do you mean you 'think' the vamp got them?"

"Sir, our scouts are dead, sir, is what he meant," the other wolf spat out in fear with some anger mixed in.

Their leader glanced over at the shifter who had spoken and then over at the wolf that he still held up against the tree. He stood back, looked around at those gathered, seeing the same mixture of fear and anger in the eyes of his men. "Alright, this has gone on long enough. No more sending small groups up against this scum. You, you and you," he said pointing to three of his bodyguards. "I want half of these men changed now and the rest armed with all the weapons that we have. We go up this mountain in half-an-hour and we kill anything that gets in our way."

All the shifters stood there for a few seconds until their leader started to growl and clap his hands together. "Now, let's move it, gentlemen, we're going on a vamp hunt. Let's get our act together before that abomination kills any more of us." With that, all the shifter's moved into high gear to follow Marcus's commands, knowing that probably many of them wouldn't live to see the next morning.

OOOOO

I sat in the big recliner, an icy cold can of diet Pepsi sitting in my hand, half drained. I was listening to the mixed group of humans and Supers plan out how they were going to use me to take back the world from the big baddies. I looked around the spacious cabin that we were in and was glad that this place had more room than the old man's other house had.

With another sip of the cold caffeine, I sighed at the loud voices hashing out plans on who would do what in this coming venture. They had been going on like this for over two hours now and no one seemed to have given an inch in compromise.

Finally getting tired of the whole deal, I drained the soda, got up, and crushing the can walked toward the kitchen table where the mixed group was gathered. No one paid me any attention until I threw the squashed soda can into their midst.

As the can spun around in the middle of the table, all eyes turned toward me as the voices died. I gave everyone my best smile as I said, "Now that I all have your attention, I would just like to remind you that you are all talking about using me without any of my input."

"It's not like we don't want your input, young lady," the old man started to say then he paused and glanced around the group then back at me. "It's just that we are all seasoned fighters, and well . . . you know you're a . . ."

I looked daggers at the old man and then at the rest. "If you or any of you say I'm just a girl then we are going to have a problem. Besides Shane is a girl and she's right in the middle of the planning."

Everyone looked at Shane and then back at me. "Well she is a fae not a girl," Michael said. Then stopped and looked back at the fae. "Sorry, that came out wrong. You know what I mean."

The fae smiled and waved away the comment. "What the human means, Ruby Red, is that we all have experience in fighting," she glanced over at the old man and the dragon then back at me. "Some have been fighting for a very long time. So until you have gained your powers and some experience, then we think it would be better if you just let us take care of the war planning."

I was going to give one nasty retort back to the fae when we all heard snarls and growls outside the cabin. I rushed to the door, hearing chairs being knocked over behind me and the dragon's voice yelling at me to stay inside. Ignoring the voices behind me, I wrenched the door open stepping onto the porch of the old man's home. The stars and what moon there was shone brightly down into the large clearing, lighting up the scene that lay before me. On one side of the open area stood two men, while across from them about fifty very large men and wolves were coming out of the woods looking none too happy to be there.

As I stepped down from the porch onto the ground, everyone in front of me froze in place as humans, and Supers alike poured out of the cabin and spread out along the porch behind me.

We all stood around like that for a few minutes until the largest of the werewolves detached himself from the group and came walking over to me. He paused about fifteen feet away when I heard Michael release the safety on his weapon. Of course, in the quiet of the night that seemed to be the only sound in the clearing since even the nighttime animals and insects were making no noise.

The shifter stood there looking me up and down and then a ghost of a smile flittered across his face. "You have her eyes, daughter."

A veil of red anger dropped over those eyes and I took a quick step forward, feeling my claws and canines start to elongate. "You do not get to talk about my mother, dog."

This brought a snicker from my side and I took a step back and glanced to my left where I saw one of the men who had been standing across the clearing now stood about ten feet away. I snarled in anger and a touch of fright that the person in front of me had moved so close to me so quietly. "And who the hell are you?"

The surfer boy smiled and gave me a little bow. "Davey, my love. My name is Davey."

"He is a vamp," my father spit out with all the hate he could muster.

I glanced over at my father and then back at the vamp who was now giving my father a murderous look. I couldn't help throwing my head back and laughing at the vamp and this snapped his head around from my father to me as a frown crossed his face. "What is so funny, my love?"

I took two steps toward the vamp and snapped out, "First thing is, I'm not your love." This declaration deepened his frown. "Second thing is, a vamp that looks like a surfer and named Davey seems pretty damn funny to me after all that has gone down the last few days."

The vamp dropped his head to look at the ground then snapped it up as a look of intense anger washed over it. "No one laughs at me, not even you, my love," the vamp hissed and in a flash, he was across the clearing standing next to the other man.

As the vamp raised his hands in the air and mumbled some words, I saw my father give a signal and the shifters that had come with him started to move across the clearing. Some moved toward the vamp while others headed in my group's direction.

Right about then the whole clearing seemed to open up and disgorge a multitude of creatures from the ground. I heard someone behind me shout 'zombies', but pretty much figured that out by myself by the smell and sight of the decayed and rotting flesh of these creatures. Of course, that is when all hell broke loose in the dark night surrounding the cabin.

With the chaos surrounding me, my eyes were drawn to the sight of one of the shifters going down in the arms of a zombie that was just coming out of the ground while two others had a death grip on his legs. Somehow the shifter made it back to his feet. Reaching down, he tried to pry one of the creatures off of his legs while the one on his back was gnawing on his neck.

I caught the quick flash of movement as one of Michael's fighters kneeled down with those impressive weapons of theirs not ten feet away from this drama and pulled the trigger. I don't know what kind of ammo those things sported but right then I promised myself I was going to get me one of those as shifter and zombies all disappeared in a mist of blood. The only thing left was the bottom half of the two zombies coming out of the ground and the shifter's lower legs. Oh hell, I really, really needed one of those, I thought.

The man's triumph was short-lived though as he stood to find another target and was bowled over by three zombies that started to eat him alive as he struggled to bring his weapon to bear on them. I took a step forward to help him when I felt an iron grip on my wrist and I was pulled into my father's chest. "And where do you think you are going, daughter dear?" I struggled to get out of his grip as I could see flashes of the fae and old man as they tried to fight their way through zombies and wolves to get to me.

I felt myself lifted off the ground and heard my father growl, "Make sure that I'm not followed," when four of the largest shifters stepped behind us and let go with some wicked weapons of their own. The wolves spread their death across the clearing, not caring who they took down. I watched as we moved down the trail as human, zombie, and shifter alike went down under their murderous barrage.

We had gone about ten feet down a trail when I raked my silver claws across my father's arms. This didn't seem to accomplish much except to get him to let out an angry roar and as he spun me around I saw a flash of his fist and then all went black.

OOOOO

I woke up as I hit the ground and all the air was knocked out of my lungs. I opened my eyes trying to suck in a breath as I glanced around at the truck that I laid next to. That's when I heard the scuffle of feet near the front tire and a quick growl. When I finally got enough air in my lungs to try and stand, I pulled myself up the side of the truck using one of the back door handles for support. I heard my father's voice snarl, "Well I see you're up, pup. Good because once I find the damn keys to this truck we are out of here and back to Seattle."

I looked over at my father as his head once more

disappeared down around the front of the truck, "I'm not going anywhere with you, I . . ."

My father's head popped up with a small black box gripped in his hand, a small satisfied smile now on his face. "Doesn't matter what you want, girl, you're coming with me whether you like it or not."

I started to move toward the back of the truck as my father came around the front, the black box was gone and the truck key dangling in his hand. The smile was replaced by a look of annoyance as I moved further away from him. "Don't make this any harder, girl, just get in the truck." He hesitated as he unlocked the door and opened it and then once more took a step toward me. "Believe me, daughter, if I have to chase you down you will regret it, just like your mother used to."

I was just about to open my mouth to reply to his statement when I saw a flash of spinning silver hit my father in the chest, propelling him into the truck door and ripping it off its hinges. The bundle of the door, my father, and his attacker flew across the clearing and slammed into another truck, rocking the vehicle on its suspension.

I watched as the small bundle of fae separated from my father and stood up. Shane stood there breathing hard as she glanced back at me and gave me a quick smile. "Hello, Ruby Red, figured you might need a little help with this dog here."

As I took a step forward, the fae glanced back at my father

but was hit by him as he came off the ground as her attention had been on me. I watched the two fly through the air once more, hitting some small trees at the edge of the clearing and disappearing into the dark night.

Someone screamed in frustration and then I fell to the ground as I felt my anger and the change overcome me. The sounds of battle were in the background as I felt my body transform into the monster that was supposed to save the world. I can say this at least the old man was right that each time the transformation happened there was less pain and it would be quicker than the one before it. For in seconds, I was once again on my feet now in the half-formed werewolf hybrid that I had been before.

Unfortunately for my father, he took that moment to walk out of the woods dragging the fae by her hair. As he hit the tree line, I saw him fling the fae's body across the clearing and saw it collide with another of his trucks.

The large sneer on his face disappeared and his eyes went wide when I gave out a loud howl while jumping over the hood of the truck. Swinging my huge paws, I connected with his head separating it from the rest of his body. His head smashed into a tree and rolled back toward me where I stomped down on that evil sphere. The feel and sound of the crunch gave me a satisfaction that brought an even louder howl out of my half-formed animal throat.

As I finished my primal night cry, I heard a whisper of sound behind me and a hand touched my shoulder in a

loving caress and I heard the vamp's voice say, "My love, I
. . ." Guess he didn't know it was a bad idea to grab a
monster that was in the middle of a killing madness.

I spun around, grabbed the vamp and flung him into the
nearest object which happened to be a large slab of rock
that stuck up out of the ground at the side of the clearing.
Hearing the crunch of his body smashing into the solid
object brought a grunt of satisfaction from my lips. I would
have probably left right there with him plastered against the
rock like a bug on the wall if he hadn't held out his hand
and whispered, "But, my love?"

I didn't give the vamp a chance to finish his declaration of
love. I had grabbed the loose door of the truck and was
standing over him, letting all my anger and frustration of
the last couple days out on his body. "I'M", {SMASH},
"NOT," {SMASH}, "YOUR," {SMASH}, "LOVE," I
yelled. Using the metal door to emphasize my words was
pretty satisfying for me. For him? Not so much, I'm
guessing.

I stopped as I heard my name shouted out by three or four
different voices. I looked around at the old man, humans,
and the dragon that was supporting an injured fae. The
only sound in the clearing that could be heard was low
moans from the rock in front of me. I glanced down at the
crushed and distorted door in my hand and dropped it and
then took a step back from the vamp and his rock.

If I thought the door was damaged and mangled, that was

nothing compared to what was stuck to the rock. Any resemblance to the blond pretty boy surfer was long gone as it looked like someone had smeared a blob of red meat sauce all over the rock. The moaning from the creature had stopped and what was left of its body slowly slid down the rock creating a nasty smear of red.

"Come on, young lady, we need to get out of here before the shifters come down off my mountain," the old man said as he laid a grizzled, gnarled old hand on my shoulder. I guess the killing feeling inside of me had died as I looked at what I had done to the vamp for I just gave a quick nod of my head and started to follow the old man away from the rock. Unfortunately for me, I only got two feet when I felt the ground rush up to meet me and all went dark.

# AFTERMATH

It's been two weeks since that night. I don't remember much after I passed out. I woke up two days later and devoured all the food in the house that we were staying in. Michael and the rest of the humans went back the next day to bury their dead and to take care of any Supers that were still around but came back with some disturbing news.

It seems that whatever was left of the vamp had been carried away and they had to take care of the few zombies that were still wandering around the old man's mountain. I guess the shifters weren't too happy with me taking out my father so they burned the old man's cabin down and did some terrible things to the human dead that had been left behind. After hearing some of the gruesome details, I guess I'll never admonish the fae for stealing a few dollars from their dead again.

Right now I am training under the three Supers: the old man, the dragon and the fae to learn as much magic as I can while Michael's band of humans are trying to gather as many allies as they can to take the fight to the leaders of the Supers. It is slow going on both fronts. I'm having trouble opening up to my powers like I did the night of the fight, and while Michael has found plenty of the downtrodden, not many are willing to put their lives or those of their families at risk. I sit at night thinking about my mother and how much I miss her and I know deep down that I don't blame them for being scared for themselves or the ones that they love.

So, for now, I train as hard as I can trying to gain my magic powers while I sit and listen to all these battle experienced veterans plan out how they are going to use their ultimate weapon— me. And what of this sister that I'm supposed to have? So far Percy won't tell me anything about her or where she is. I can only hope that wherever she is this madness has not touched her life yet.

# EPILOGUE – THE SISTER

The little girl shifts in her dungeon room as the chains that hold her to the wall rattle scrapping bruised skin and causing old wounds to open and seep out pus and blood. She ignores the tiny vermin that live on her body as they bite and move in places that she as long ago stopped scratching. The sound of marching feet and the sight of the flickering light in the darkness of the queen's dungeon makes her peek out from under the nest of red hair that nearly covers her entire face.

"Well hello, my dear," a thin high voice whispers in the little light that spills through her cage door. She moves not a muscle, staying curled up in a ball still peeking out from the rat's nest of her hair.

The tall, thin silver-haired lady stands there for a few seconds then turns to one of the small child's jailers. "Is the abomination still alive?"

"Yes mistress, at least when we put food in the cage it is

eaten," he says with a quick shrug.

The queen looks down at the jailer until he bows and then steps back from the door. She then turns and looks down at the small bundle huddled on the floor. "Well, never mind. I doubt that this place could kill you anyways. But I did want you to know that your sister has come into her powers and we will have need of you, little one."

The queen turns to one of her court guards and smiles. "Take this thing, clean her up and get her fed. I want her ready to start her training."

The guard nods and then stops as he starts to open the cage. "And who should fill the cage, if we take her out, my Queen?"

The queen looks around at all the faces surrounding her. They all know her standing rule – none of her dungeons shall ever stand empty. Her smile brightens as she looks at the jailer and points at him. "Oh hell, throw him in. He seems pretty worthless." With that, she turns with the rest of her entourage and marches out of the dark dungeons as one prisoner is exchanged for another.

## ABOUT THE AUTHOR

Robert Wright is the author of the "Witch Way" series, books written as young adult/fantasy. Never one to stay with a single idea, he is also the author of the young adult/sci-fi series, "Walk the Stars". The second book in the series, "Walk the Earth", is in progress and will be coming out Spring, 2017. Also in the works is the continuation of the Others world introduced in the "Witch Way" series. "Into Darkness" will introduce the "Demon Child" series planned for Summer, 2017.

His characters are based on drawings and doodles that he has worked on since he could pick up a pencil. Robert has traveled the world and met many interesting people but now lives in Bellingham, Washington with his wife and youngest child (along with his imaginary friend Percy, the dragon). Bellingham is the setting for "Witch Way Back" as well as "Ruby Red and the Wolf" and other planned "Ruby Red" books. For more information on these enjoyable books please visit witchwaybooks.com or stop by the Witch Way Books page on Facebook.

Made in the USA
Columbia, SC
28 July 2021